TEN SECONDS

1 9 9 1

LOUIS

GRAYWOLF PRESS / SAINT PAUL

TEN

SECONDS

EDWARDS

To Sherman Edmiston

All the best,

Louis Edwards

Publication of this volume is made possible in part by grants from the Jerome
Foundation; the Minnesota State Arts Board, with funds provided through an
appropriation by the Minnesota State Legislature; and the National Endowment
for the Arts. Graywolf Press is the recipient of a McKnight Foundation Award
administered by the Minnesota State Arts Board and receives generous
contributions from corporations, foundations, and individuals. Graywolf Press
is a member agency of United Arts, Saint Paul.

Publication of this book is made possible with additional support provided
by the Jerome Foundation.

"My Girl," written by William Robinson/Ronald White, copyright © 1964,
used by permission of Jobete Music Co., Inc. "Redemption Song," Bob Marley
Music Ltd., copyright © 1980, used by permission of PolyGram/Island Music
Publishing Group.

Published by GRAYWOLF PRESS
2402 University Avenue
Saint Paul, Minnesota 55114
All rights reserved

9 8 7 6 5 4 3 2
First printing, 1991
A paperback original

Library of Congress Cataloging-in-Publication Data

Edwards, Louis, 1962–
        Ten seconds / Louis Edwards.
            p.   cm.
        ISBN 1-55597-150-4 (pbk.) : $8.95
        I. Title
        PS3555.D945T46   1991
        813'.54 – dc20   90-24659

To my mother, Faye Lockett

To my sister, Marla Reed

And to Dwayne Patrick Aaron

Hold to the now, the here, through
which all future plunges to the past.

James Joyce, *Ulysses*

None but ourselves can free our minds.

Bob Marley, "Redemption Song"

I

THE RACE

FRIDAY, APRIL 24, 1981

EDDIE was twenty-six years old, and he was thinking about how he didn't really mind these arguments with Betty. After over six years of marriage he had come to understand them as something that came with a Jake-and-cake. That was the way he and his buddies referred to a wedding. The term went all the way back to when they were in high school. Junior year. That was the year that Sandra Baker, a cheerleader, turned up pregnant in the middle of the basketball season and Jake Harmon was pronounced the guilty party. Quiet little Jake. And he and Sandra were forced into getting married immediately. At the wedding reception Eddie, Malcolm, and some of the other groomsmen were standing in a corner of the Knights of Peter Claver Hall drinking

champagne when they looked up at the long elaborately decorated table and saw Jake standing there alone, looking lost. He
stood next to a gigantic wedding cake that reached the level of his
brow. Someone called his name, and Jake turned quickly in re-
sponse, in the process swiping a dot of white icing with his nose.
The guys all howled with a laughter laced with an incipient sense
for tragedy and pathos, and "Jake-and-cake" immediately moved
into their vernacular.

Benefits of a Jake-and-cake included children – two for Eddie, a
girl and a boy, ages three and five; sex, obviously, though not with
too much more freedom now than prior to the Jake-and-cake (he
had had the fantasy of waking up at all hours of the morning, finding the familiar hard warm knot below his belly, and just rolling
over and drowning himself in his private Caribbean; but Betty – a
woman who was no one's ocean and who, in fact because of her
honesty and air of spirituality, reminded most people of the sky –
had told him the morning after his first and last such venture,
quite calmly and in a faraway voice as she moved in what seemed
to him slow motion, toward him with her right arm extending a
steaming hot pot of grits, presumably to serve him breakfast, "I
love you, but don't you ever do what you did last night again. I feel
like a horse," and him, hearing her words but not listening to
them – thinking so loudly, oh, how many black men before him,
because of some misjudgment on the part of the knot below the
belly, had seen this same pot of grits – not listening to the words
but knowing precisely what she was saying); and arguments, like
the one they had just had. It was another stupid one about his for-
getting to pay a bill, or his not cutting the grass, or not checking
the oil or transmission fluid in her Toyota like he was supposed to,
or about the whites of his eyes being too red because he was drinking too much liquor or cuz he was smoking so much of that ole
stuff, and you couldn't call yourself nobody's daddy when your
eyes were *that* red; the arguments overlapped and intertwined in
his mind and had over the years accumulated and woven them-

selves into an impenetrable gauzy gray veil that dropped over all thought any time Betty said his name with the same inflection she used when she scolded Tammy and Edward Junior, so that each new argument would be a brief period of numbness that, upon its conclusion, instead of causing him grief or anguish, gave him a sense of rejuvenation, a fresh way of looking at the world, as though he had awakened from a healthful rest or as though he were a blind man just given sight. Colors became brighter, milk didn't upset his stomach, and sometimes sex was like drowning marvelously in a private ocean. So he'd let her go on with whatever she was talking about, because he knew pleasure would soon follow. All would be fine soon. One day she would beat him home from work, and the mailman would have delivered a note from the utility company saying "Thank you for your payment," and reading that probably would have made her feel so comfortable, secure and proud, having accomplished what she saw as the remarkable achievement of being just a regular American, paying her bills and everything, how good it was to be in the mainstream of America – if only for a second – how good it was to be in step when it was so easy to be out of step, when she was black and everyone expected her to be out of step anyway (but she was showing them now, if only for a second, she was showing them now), how lucky she was to be making it when her cousins wrote bad checks and were on a first-name basis with the sweet-speaking, shrill-speaking people from collection agencies (here she'd make the sign of the cross and thank God Eddie was adequate, only adequate but a hero nevertheless), oh, how lucky she was. Yes, that was how she felt, he knew, for she was singing while she cooked and he'd peek at the notepad on the refrigerator door and see tacked there the envelope with a big blue check mark on it. All was fine. And that night they would make love and afterward talk about the world in such detail that they would startle themselves with how deeply they thought and felt and how much they knew; they would tell their secrets because it was okay to tell your secrets to someone who felt that deeply and knew that much about things. Betty told Eddie about how when she was sixteen and her baby sister, Coco, was fifteen, Coco had waked her late one night in the bed they shared and told her that she had missed her period and was probably pregnant. She begged Betty to help her but not to tell Mama, and she was crying so horribly and making such a mess on the pillow that Betty had agreed. There had been an abortion, and Mama never knew. But something had gone wrong and the doctor told Coco she could never have children. Betty cried as she told Eddie her story, confessing her deep feelings of guilt. She should have told Mama about Coco, but she had been silly and childish and let Coco swear her to secrecy. And here she was, guilty again, telling him the secret she'd sworn never to tell, when she hadn't even told Mama like she should have. But she was glad to have him there to tell it to, and Eddie believed her when she said it, because as she said it, she began gripping both his biceps with that painfully tight hold that babies use to grip index fingers and she was pulling herself so close to him, as though she were trying to crawl all under his skin, her long nails threatening to cut him and give her an opening. And later that same night she asked him to tell her how he lost his virginity. "Who was it?" she giggled, touching him playfully. "I don't care." Kind, the way she used only the palm of her hand, aware of her dangerous nails. Too kind for him. He was silent; she had to ask him again, still giggling, a flowing chuckle of innocence. And he told her something about Belinda Travis and about a wooded area someplace and about the back of somebody's pickup truck and about there having been no pleasure; he couldn't remember the details of the lie. But he'd had to lie. (Thank God Edward Junior, who was not yet two years old at that time, had screamed out from his room just then, because Eddie had started to stutter, making it all up as he went along.) How could he, with Betty's tear stains still on his chest, tell her about him and Coco? How could he ever tell her

6

that? After that night, for the two months immediately preceding winter, the leaves were raked and the grass was always cut.

But that had happened so long ago that it all seemed like a dream. Right now Eddie just wanted the numbness to go away, for new thoughts to have a chance, so he left the house, hearing himself mumble to Betty that he'd be home by ten and hearing Tammy crying to go with him. "I wanna go with Daddy, Mama. I want some donuts."

He got into his dusty green El Camino and drove away, humming along with the staticky AM radio he never turned off. He had to slow down briefly to allow two children who were playing tennis in the street to step aside, then he drove on – noticing, but not really noticing, the row of houses (how many, he couldn't guess) on either side of the street. They were only shadowy colored figures, brown and beige squares, red and white triangles. ("Brown!" Tammy, who was just beginning to learn her colors at the time, had yelled once as they passed Mark and Debra's place. "The top of our house is like a triangle, Daddy," Edward Junior had said recently.) There had to be people in the yards or on the porches to give the houses meaning. He knew Almeta Landry, the old lady who lived on the corner, would be sitting in a rocking chair on her front porch. And since he hated the way she made him feel whenever his eyes met hers, he looked straight ahead at the stop sign. There was something eerie about Almeta. She always made him think about a scary movie he used to see all the time on the late, late show when he was a boy. Something about little girls making prank telephone calls and saying to the person on the other end, "I know who you are and I saw what you did." That used to scare Eddie when he was ten and twelve and fourteen. It always seemed to him that no matter who answered the phone, that person must have done something wrong. Every time he watched the movie, he had either just stolen a dollar off his parents' dresser or just smoked a cigarette or a joint with Malcolm

7

in the backyard or just let the Nasty Man act like he was showing him how to do it with a girl when he knew all the time that the man just wanted to play with his thing. His own mischief had made that movie one of the scariest he had ever seen. And Almeta Landry was just like those little girls. Whenever she spoke to you from her porch, that dingy old black and orange crocheted shawl wrapped around her shoulders, her eyes glanced up from the Bible in her lap, through gray hairs, and said, "I know who you are and I saw what you did." Eddie turned the corner by her house onto Vincent Road and watched the dusky sky.

Vincent Road ran along I-210, the freeway that jutted off of I-10 and curved its way around the city of South End. It was I-210 that Eddie used to get to and from the oil refinery where he worked; it provided a bridge across Lake Jordan to Lakeside, the small town where several oil and chemical plants had located to take advantage of the rich oil reserves and easy access to the Gulf of Mexico. South End, a city with a population of about 90,000, provided most of the work force for the plants. Eddie loved the drive on I-210 to work. It was such a breeze. He drove it at fifty miles per hour, just before a rattle would start under the hood of his car. The way coming back was slower – traffic was heavier – but that just meant that he had more time to think. Everyone he knew took the van pool to save money, but he didn't care about the money. And, besides, his car didn't burn much gas. But even if it did, he wouldn't be willing to give up the ride across the lake twice a day. Somehow it soothed him. Malcolm, his best friend, who worked at the same refinery, had ridden with him for a while, but that didn't last long. Having someone else in the car, even Malcolm, bothered Eddie. The presence of another person seemed to be some sort of intrusion. And one day he had snapped at Malcolm. Told him, more or less, to shut up. He had told Malcolm, who could almost never be accused of talking too much, to shut up. On this particular day, Malcolm wasn't really saying much at all. It was just that what he was saying wasn't amounting to anything. A lot of and's and uh's and you know's. He might have been trying to say something important, but this time his talent for brief, quiet eloquence was failing him; all Eddie could hear was a jumble of nothings. And all the while Malcolm was rambling there was the yearning to experience the therapeutic crossing of the lake in silence. So he had raised his voice a little and said he was tired, and in their private system of communication he had just told Malcolm to shut up. He had caught the twitch at the corner of Malcolm's eye that followed the announcement of his fatigue, a twitch of such deep disappointment that it might have paved the way for the first wrinkle, a twitch of indignation and quick decision. He had not been surprised when, a few days later, Malcolm had come to him with an excuse about feeling guilty because Eddie wouldn't take any gas money and said he was going to go back to the van pool. Eddie offered to take a few dollars a week, but Malcolm's mind was made up. This was one time, however, that his stubbornness didn't bother Eddie one bit. He preferred to ride alone, really. You just couldn't carry on a conversation while you crossed the bridge. You couldn't even sing along with the radio.

Eddie came to a stop at the red light at the intersection of Vincent Road and Cameron Highway, which, only about thirty-five miles down to the south, ended where the Gulf of Mexico began. Eddie sat, waiting for the light to change, and played the game of watching the flashing red and yellow turn-signal lights of the cars across from him until they flashed on and off together, the right-turn signal of the car on his left and the left-turn signal of the car on his right. Watching the lights was Betty's game; he never came up with things like that. He had caught her playing it one day a couple of years ago. She told him that the object of the game was to catch the lights flashing together as many times as you could before the traffic light turned green. She warned that it was virtually impossible to do it even twice; she'd been able to do so only once. "But," he had asked, "what's the point?" She had shrugged. "It's something to do. When you catch them together, it just makes you feel good." But the few times that he had played the game since then and had managed to catch the lights flashing together, he had not experienced the good feeling that Betty had spoken of. He had even seen the lights flash together twice, and he still didn't know what she meant when she said that the lights flashing together made her feel good. To him the game was just a way to kill a little time. Now, as he was sitting watching the lights flash irregularly, he heard someone behind him honk that it was time to go. He crossed Cameron Highway and glided into the left-turn lane that would put him on the entrance ramp to I-210. He stopped briefly, then moved across more to the left, onto the ramp, slowly picking up speed, on his way to fifty.

To the southwest, about two miles away in the distance, he saw the stadium lights on at South End High, and he immediately remembered that the school was hosting a track meet. The sports pages had been filled with stories about the teams coming in from Texas and about how the local Louisiana teams would be up against their toughest competition of the season. A color photograph from the newspaper showing a high jumper dressed in a red top and blue trunks caught in the air above the bar and the blue landing pit had stayed in Eddie's mind since this morning. (Photographs had always impressed him as being magical somehow. All kinds of photographs, but mainly those that could be called action shots. He was still fascinated by a picture his mother had of him as a baby, in which he was reaching playfully for his big toe. It looked just like him and, though he couldn't explain why, it made him feel both happy and sad.) The photograph in the newspaper had reminded him of his own high school track and field days when he had been a star sprinter and Malcolm had been a standout in the field. Darrell something-or-other was the name beneath the photograph. He was picked to win the high jump, and his team was the reigning Texas state champion. In the photograph Darrell, poised above the bar, looked like an exotic bird someone had shot, who was about to land quietly in a square blue pond – with all his dreams about singing tomorrow morning and searching for and eating worms and insects and mating, about sitting in a nest surrounded by eggs, then rapidly developing wings, then insolence, then sad farewells, with all these dreams tucked in his red breast; with his eyes closed tightly and his beak open to the sky. The picture had made some simple and barely felt connection for Eddie as he had stared at it this morning in a caffeine-nicotine daze. It represented, he knew, a single moment – motion stopped, time stopped. But he had endowed it with the quality of continuity, perhaps even to the point of infinity. At the moment captured in the picture, Darrell was there above the bar. But not long before, he had been on the ground, and not long after he would be in the blue. There had been a before; there would be an after. The picture was only now. But there was always a before and always an after. Always. Eddie felt a compulsion to be at the track meet. He wanted to see something, to feel something, though he wasn't quite sure just what. Something to do with Darrell maybe. Or maybe it was because he thought Malcolm would be there and probably some of the other guys. He would be able to have a little fun and afterward go home, carried by the rejuvenated feeling, and make up with Betty. He remembered the caption below the picture: "Darrell ——— will fly high tonight at 6:30." He looked at his watch; it was already 7:25. He sped toward the stadium at nearly sixty miles per hour, enduring the rattle, hoping to make it there in time to see Darrell in flight.

*   *   *

BY TRACK MEET standards, the crowd was large, Eddie had to park so far out in the stadium parking lot that his jog to the entrance gate left him gasping a little for breath. He paid the three-dollar admission charge and walked up the concrete ramp to the wooden bleachers. Turning to face the audience, he was wide-eyed, hoping to spot immediately some of his friends. When he didn't, he felt a little twinge of disappointment, but he knew that if he climbed higher up and looked down and scanned the entire audience he would be able to spot some of the guys. So he hopped up to the upper rows of the bleachers and found a seat. And just as he thought, looking down he could see he wasn't alone, because there below, about fifteen rows down in the middle of the section to his left, were Nutty and Charlie clowning – yelling so loudly at each other that Eddie could almost hear them, Charlie wearing that grimy Pepsi cap he got for taking a taste test at 7-Eleven, Nutty waving a ten-dollar bill, no doubt wanting to bet that he was in the right in their argument. Sitting near Nutty and Charlie were Booker and Hank, two Jake-and-cake veterans, both with their kids gathered around them. Booker's five-year-old, Ricky, sat facing the crowd, his back to the track, blowing bubbles the size of oranges with his gum. Eddie continued to look across the audience in search of familiar faces (he was sure Malcolm was in the crowd someplace), but before he could recognize anyone else, he remembered Darrell, the one he'd come to see, and looked to his right, to the north, just beyond the end zone of the football field where the high jump pit was always set up for track meets, but there were no athletes in the area. Eddie's heart dropped. The event must have already ended. It wasn't even eight o'clock yet, but it had ended. Damn! He had missed it. The urge he had felt to be down there hanging out with the guys and having fun (an urge somehow intensified by the way a single bubble had exploded in a burst of joy all over little Ricky's expectant face) subsided. He let himself settle into his seat; he didn't want to be with them right now. Then suddenly, for the moment, they were blocked completely from his mind. All he could think about was the something he had missed, something vital, it seemed to him. And then again suddenly – beads of sweat began to appear on his forehead and to glisten in the dying sunlight. A fear came over him that he did not understand. It chilled him. It told him that he couldn't go home, that he couldn't even move. It threatened to break up the rhythm of his life – not only the rhythm of his life now, but the rhythm of his memories of the past and of his dreams of the future. And it was all because he'd missed something. But missed what? It had to be more than missing the high jumping event that was making him feel this regretful, that was making him feel that going home would be impossible. What had he missed? He heard the answer whispered into his ear: *Anything. Anything.* He felt that if he blinked his eyes, he couldn't go home. He needed to feel it all. If he didn't see red and blue and if he didn't hear screams and laughter and applause, didn't taste victory and defeat, he couldn't go home. Not tonight. And he'd already missed something, the thing he'd come to see. He couldn't go home. Who would comfort Betty tonight? His mind was confused, busy, trying to catch everything, trying to catch color, sound, feeling. In echoes the announcer's voice came to him over the loudspeaker saying that the next-next race-race was to be the hundred-hundred meter-meter dash-dash. Hundred-meter-hundred-dash-meter-hundred-meter-dash-dash. He watched and listened closely as the world seemed to come at him in waves. He watched the athletes jogging on the track, warming up, stretching, shaking hands, smiling, saying "Good luck, man" and "That's some tough spikes, bro" and "I'm gon be burnt for my relay" and "Weren't you in *Sports Illustrated* last week?" Yes, they must be saying things like that. Eddie was guessing. He had to guess. Somehow he had to make up for what he had missed. He wanted to be able to go home. So he had to take everything in, to make up for what he had missed. Every sight, every sound, every moment.

The announcer was calling the names of the runners in the race. "In lane number one is Michael Briggins of Lafayette High," he said. "And in lane number two, Richard Welcome from Westlake. Ronald Baker, who ran the last leg on Taft's winning 400-meter relay team, is in lane number three. In lane four is Warren Tisdale of Q. D. Jacob High. And in lane number five, Central's Darrell McDaniel." And there he was. Darrell. Not something-or-other, but McDaniel. Darrell McDaniel in a red top and blue trunks, in lane number five, jogging in place, flapping his arms, trying to loosen up. He was taller and skinnier than the others, with very dark skin, and his inch-long hair looked kinky and damp. He had placed first in the high jump, the announcer informed the audience. ("In lane number six is Kevin McKay from Wheatley High.") Darrell had a weary, exhausted look about him, as though the humid southwestern Louisiana air had saturated his body and was weighing him down. ("In lane number seven is Patrick Dodds from LaGrange.") Perspiration sparkled on his black skin under the stadium lights, which were gradually replacing the sun, and wetness soaked through in patches on his tank top. ("And Cedric Jones of Catholic rounds out the field in lane eight.") Eddie saw thick veins in Darrell's arms and legs and maybe (he wasn't sure, but maybe) blood at the back of his left calf where he must have spiked himself. He felt certain that the kid didn't have a chance and wondered why his coach hadn't scratched him from the race. But the race was about to begin. There in the infield, about ten yards from the runners, was the starter: a fat man with a gun. He called them to their marks, and the runners took their places at the starting line. And set... *Pow!*

Pow-Pow! The gun fired quickly twice more, and the runners all began to slow down upon hearing the extra shots that meant a runner had jumped the gun, started illegally, and was disqualified from the race. A man with a red flag raised in his right hand stepped into lane five; Darrell had jumped too soon and was out of the race. He moved sluggishly toward the infield, but in some way he seemed relieved to Eddie. He walked slowly across the football field to the high jump area, while the other runners were lining up, taking their marks. The starter told the runners to get set, and as they did so, Darrell started a little jog toward the blue landing pit, pretending to approach for a jump. In the silence that waited for the race to begin, he planted his right foot and jumped high, arching his back gracefully over an invisible bar. And as the gun went *Pow!* to start the race, Darrell collapsed, began his descent into the blue pond at the north end of the field. For Eddie, there was only this: the *Pow!* and the falling into the blue. But there was everything in the *Pow!* and the falling and the blue. Every sight, every sound, every moment. The *Pow!* fit perfectly into a deep, dark hole of personal silence, as though it were the last piece to a jigsaw puzzle of his soul; the falling and the blue blended together to form moving images sharper than those of even the best dreams. He felt that he was suspended in the heart of a tornado, in the eye of a hurricane, and the chaos of his existence was spiraling around him. He was seeing colors, he was hearing whispers, he was raising his hands, snapping his fingers, kicking out his left leg, staring out windows, tying laces, opening doors; his soul was feeling warm, hot, cool, cold, and warm again – quickly. The feelings were both precious and scary, and there was nothing he could do to stop them. Life rushed past the light of his mind's eye at a rate of so many frames per second, with the breadth of so many millimeters per frame.

And he was seventeen, a boy in the heat of his own private, confused passion; he was twenty-six, sitting here feeling this; and he was thirty-five, nine years in the future. He had not lived it, but he was sure it would happen. Yes, there it was. Nine years from now he would be at home on a Sunday afternoon watching television – football if it was fall, basketball if it was spring, and Betty would come into the living room with a look on her face like the one she had when all was fine, while he was watching someone, Dr. J, dribbling the ball fast up the court against a single defender (it was spring) – but no, no, it was not Dr. J; it was someone different, younger. So he'd be watching someone else, but it was basketball and it was the Seventy-Sixers and it was spring. Betty was moving toward him. ("Doesn't he remind you of Julius Erving, the great one-on-one ability, the sudden flash of excitement!" "Yes, you're so right, J. B.") The Seventy-Sixers – no, uhn-uhn, not the Seventy-Sixers at all, just a red jersey, red like a matador's

flag, and a number on the jersey that was not Dr. J's number six
(6) but some function of six with a three in it, possibly $3 + 3$ (33),
or 3×2 (32), or 2×3 (23) – and she'd come in down the hall
from the bedroom and stand there with that look on her face like
on the good nights and block the screen, in the middle of a fast
break, blocking the screen, then bending, unbuckling his belt,
unzipping his pants, then kneeling, not blocking the screen anymore, her head somewhere below his belly. And he'd see that
someone, that not – Dr. J someone, 23 on the instant replay, glid-
ing through the air, slam dunking the ball hard through the hoop.
Then he'd see it again from all the angles – the half-court diagonal
view, the behind-the-glass shot, the slow-motion replay. Jam,
jam, jam. In your face. (" . . . the sudden flash of excitement!")
Yes, you're so right, J. B. You are so right. And then, just when his
muscles tensed, when he gripped the chair with his left hand (his
right one was busy), when his tongue pressed hard against the
roof of his mouth, just then he would realize that he was in this
room all alone. There was no one below his belly. No Betty. Only a
knot and his hand. Where was she? Gone. But where and why
and for how long? What had he done to make her go? He must
have done something wrong. This was a terrible, empty feeling, a
feeling he'd had for a while now. (She'd been gone a long time, a
year, he knew. Just over a year.) What a mess. He was crying and
what a mess. He had to wash his hands; he had to wipe off the
chair, maybe wipe off the carpet, if some had been wasted there.
What a mess, what an empty mess. If she would only come back.
But she wouldn't; he had tried. And she had already been gone a
year. Before long, two years would have passed, then three, then
four, then five – and here, while sadly counting years, counting
time, Eddie would be overcome with the sudden, quick knowl-
edge that he had seen this all before. The whole scene. The look
on Betty's face as she approached him in a fantasy, the basketball
player dunking the ball, the muscles tensing, the gripping the
chair, the empty feeling, the tears, the mess, the mess. He had

seen it all before, a long time ago in something like a dream, in something that went whoosh and swish and splash, when he was twenty-six maybe, or when he was seventeen. But he'd seen it all before.

And now cheers, laughter and applause, were breaking out close to him. The race was coming to an end. He began to fight to hold on to everything, but the moments were leaving quickly, blurring, fading. He glimpsed unlit birthday candles. A whiff, gumbo. A fragment: shaking spears . . . Shakespeare. He couldn't hold on to everything. (He had already lost the moment when he was thirty-five and realized that he had lost Betty forever; only a vague feeling of loss remained.) He was thinking, as he struggled with the moments (he was about to be only twenty-six again), not thinking, really – sensing, rather, for surely this was not a thought: This was how the prophets did it. They took in everything all the time. If Isaiah had really seen some part of the future, this was how he had done it. Eddie felt that in some small but significant way he could understand the prophets. Should he be crying? Should being able to understand the prophets make him cry? (*He felt:* He would lose something dear to him in the future. Betty? She was the dearest thing in the world to him. Would he lose Betty? He didn't know, just a vague feeling. But the loss had something to do with a woman, he knew. A woman or at least something feminine. Perfume, soft skin, submissive eyes shying away, knowing eyes cutting toward. Betty? An old woman in orange and black? Little girls? "I know who you are –" He'd done something wrong. Yes. But what? Something having to do with a woman. Coco? He didn't know, but he had done something wrong. Would it cause him to lose Betty? Would losing her make him cry? He didn't know.) Here he was understanding the prophets, but he wasn't crying. A child would be crying. A woman would be crying. (I do that sometimes, he thought. I feel the way women feel. Sometimes sex makes me feel like a horse. Was that enough, though, for sex to make you feel like a horse sometimes?

Was that enough? No. If it were, wouldn't he be crying?)
Prophets – who certainly could feel as women feel, if indeed many
of them weren't women – had cried oceans, rivers, lakes, and
ponds. But he wasn't crying; he wasn't a prophet, even though he
sometimes felt the way women feel. What do you call that? some
part of him wondered. There must be a word for it. What do you
call it when a man can feel like that? He felt that if he had asked
this question just a split second earlier, while he was still in the
realm of the prophets (it had slipped away so quickly), the answer
would have come to him. It would have been given to him, spelled
out right before his eyes. Even now he could see the letter A. But
what was the next letter? An M or an N perhaps. But it was fading;
the moments were leaving. (Still, again, *he felt*: Another loss. Oh,
no. It was not feminine, and it was darker and even more definite,
final. A fall, a falling. Oh, no. His mind was close to it now – always close to it somehow – yet he couldn't see it, his inward view
blurred by an intense, complicated pride, his attention suddenly
diverted to his cheek, which, kissed by a hot, invisible tear, was
unexpectedly burning. Oh, no.) And as his eyes began to focus on
the runners and then on Darrell in the blue landing pit, he had,
deep in his chest, a feeling of discontent with the fast-
approaching present; however, this feeling struck him as ephem-
eral, because he could sense it being forced to give way to an
insistent, unfamiliar satisfaction, accompanied, perhaps, by even
a smile.

Looking at the runners, he saw that somebody was about to
cross the finish line. Two faceless boys, close together.

Eddie felt planted in the position where he was now standing in
the stadium. But he also felt as if he had just traveled a great distance. He could see himself walking down the bleachers, stopping to joke with Nutty and Charlie and the others, jogging to his
car, humming with the radio, stopping at a bakery to buy some
donuts for Tammy, and going home. (Yes, he could go home
now.) That was something like what he felt, but not quite. It was

more like what he sometimes felt while driving his car home from work. He would be sailing down the exit ramp off I-210 that let him off on Cameron Highway, and his heart would swell and blood wouldn't flow correctly and he'd become dizzy – all because for one brief second he had pretended that he was about to make a right turn and drive about thirty-five miles southward to the Gulf, because he had imagined himself whizzing down all the way to the end of Cameron Highway, where he would see wide-open water spreading to the south and to the east. He'd see ships with their sails rising high against the sky, and aboard the ships, which were drifting out to sea, men who looked like his relatives. "Wait!" he would yell to them. They would wave to him to hurry. "Come," the one in charge, his Uncle Raymond, would say, motioning with his bright green cap. Eddie would wade out in the direction of the nearest ship, but he would sense the futility of his efforts; the ship was moving too quickly. "Go on," he would shout. "I'll follow you. I know another way. I'll go down right here. I know how to do that. I can go under right here, and I'll meet you on the other side." The men, drifting farther and farther away, would wave good-bye to him. Gradually the water would start to overtake him. He'd chant to himself in a loud, childlike whisper: "Surrender, surrender, surrender." But just as he was going under, the dream would fade away – as he moved into the left-turn lane, homeward. But that brief, dizzy feeling, a feeling he called hope – and hope must have been the thing that was ushering in his smile – was close to the travel-feeling he felt now as he stood in the stadium. The feeling that he had actually been transported someplace without physically having moved. And he knew that this travel-feeling had something to do with the race he was watching. He had traveled with the race, but he didn't know how. It had started and it was about to end; but, in between, there had been something. At the beginning there had been Darrell falling into the blue and a *Pow!* But that couldn't take you anyplace, could it? That was just motion and color and sound. That couldn't

TEN SECONDS

take you anyplace. You were still here. You just sat and watched
the race. You sat, watched the race, stood up for the finish, and
thought about...nothing, really. Surely you thought about
something (he couldn't imagine what), but it couldn't be anything that really mattered. It couldn't be enough to account for
this rhapsodic travel-feeling, could it? It was only enough
thought to fill up the amount of time it took these guys to run a
100-meter dash. Only about ten seconds. That was all. That was
all he'd forgotten. He'd lost a zillion times that much thought
when the veil dropped with Betty.

And the two boys were crossing the finish line almost simulta-
neously, their breezes making it quiver with an odd rhythm,
whipping it back and forth, forth and back, back and forth.

SLOW-MOTION

INSTANT REPLAY

> A current under sea
> Picked his bones in whispers. As he rose and fell
> He passed the stages of his age and youth
> Entering the whirlpool.
>
> T. S. Eliot, *The Waste Land*

: □ 1

NOTE : All of the timings herein were made using hand-held instruments and thus should be considered only approximate and unofficial.

AND HE WAS 27 YEARS OLD...

HE IS standing at the back entrance to the shop. He has just walked in from the field. The shop is a big tin shed of a building where the machinists do their work and where all of the craftsmen – carpenters, pipefitters, welders, and machinists, too – have their lockers, a place where they all congregate when they're on breaks, during any free time. The workers call it "the house." When it is almost quitting time, a man still in the field might look at his watch and say to his partner, "Let's head for the house." The ceiling is high above, so the shop isn't nearly as hot as it might be. The floor is a deep gray marble-smooth concrete. A long ten-foot-wide path runs north-south through the middle of the shop, front to back. The north half of the shop, the front end, the end closest to the entrance gate of the refinery, is mainly the locker area. There are pale green benches about eighteen inches off the floor placed in front of each row of lockers. The men sit here and drink coffee from Styrofoam cups and tell jokes during the breaks. Another path runs east-west, dividing this area from the machinists' work area. This walkway leads to an air-conditioned trailer outside, on the west side of the shop, about twenty yards away across a gravel lot where the workers pick up their paychecks every other Tuesday. To the east, this walkway leads to double doors that open to a dark, stuffy hall that turns to the right. About midway down the hall on the left are the restrooms; at the end is light – the lunchroom. The south half of the shop is the area where the machinists work. It is a danger area. Even if there were no caution signs, drilling sounds, buzz-ing saws, or shooting sparks and flying iron filings, the missing fingers would be warning enough. The wide garagelike rear en-trance, the one Eddie has reached, places you right in this area. He has been standing, just outside the shop, kicking gravel. His eyes have been staring down for a few seconds through safety glasses at his black work boots, following them as they move like the feet of a procrastinating child, one digging under the rocky surface, then the other swinging lightly over the gravel, both be-coming coated with the floury gravel dust. He is afraid to look up (though he knows he is about to) and into the machinists' area, where they are still working (there are still a few minutes before the last break). He is afraid that if he looks up he will see all kinds of ugly memories. He will see what resembles to him a kind of war zone. A scene complete with a frightening clamor, buddies fall-ing, and teamwork with an obscured purpose. To him it is not a house; it is a hell. (When someone in the field says to him, "Let's go to the house," he thinks to himself, "Okay, if we must, let's go to hell.") If he looks up he will not see men smiling beneath hard hats and behind safety glasses saying "Howdy" like in the films they show sometimes. He will see men struggling. Men fighting for survival. He will see blood. The blood of those who did not make it. Men like Malcolm. Malcolm fell so quietly, they told Eddie later, that it must have been five minutes before Moonie looked down and saw him lying still, unconscious on the floor, blood oozing from the hole in his chest made by a drill bit as thick as a finger. "Jesus!" Moonie yelled. "Somebody help me! Somebody help me!" No one heard him over the din and through the earplugs, but his arms were flailing so wildly that he drew Clem Landry's attention. Clem rushed over to where Malcolm lay, followed quickly by Roger Hebert, Joe Phillips, and the rest of the shop. Then the place was complete madness. Screaming. Men running to Safety to get the doctor and the nurse. Others hurrying to tell the foremen who were in their offices at the two front corners of the shop. The blood was beginning to spread across the floor, so the crowd around Malcolm kept a five-foot radius between him and themselves. They were silent. Some of them exchanged glances with one another, then they looked over at Roger Hebert, the senior machinist under whom Malcolm was an apprentice. They shook their heads. Hadn't the dumb-ass shown the man how to operate the fuckin' drill properly? Probably not, knowing him. Yep, it looked like another classic fuck-up by old R. H. He hadn't long ago taken his own left index finger and two years ago his pinky on the same hand. Johnny Dixon always told the story about how R. H. had once tried to use a welder's torch to cut some old scrap metal to take home from the plant, and he had somehow managed to burn his right foot in half. R. H. always swore that the ugly, crescent-shaped scar on his right forearm was from when he was in the war, but no one believed him. And now this. This was too much for even old R. H. A lot of guys didn't have fingers, but they had never killed anybody. And there was no doubt: Malcolm was dead.

Moonie was apparently the only one who thought about Eddie out in the field not knowing. He waited for the doctor to get there, confirm things, and send for the ambulance, then whispered to his foreman that he was going out to tell Eddie. Moonie, a good old guy, pushing fifty. Just about the only one Eddie thought didn't have "nigger" on the tip of his tongue. (The graffiti on the bathroom walls told you what they were thinking.) They had worked together a couple of times on the same jobs, Eddie helping to reconnect some engines Moonie had repaired. They got along well. Once, Moonie even sat with Malcolm and Eddie at one of the black tables in the lunchroom. It was no big deal, didn't make anybody give any funny looks their way or anything like that. It was just that nobody ever did it. But Moonie was different. He had picked up on the friendship between Eddie and Malcolm and wanted Eddie to find out as soon as possible.

Eddie was out at the Cat Cracker removing the giant nuts that held on the heads of the filtering vessels, so that the lines and the screens could be cleaned out. He fought with the hydraulic wrench that clack-clacked away at the stubborn nuts. Sweat drained from his forehead into his eyes, blurring his vision. Only eleven o'clock and already hot as hell. The acid air of the plant made it hard for him to breathe. He felt he would never get used to this air. He'd been working here for seven years, and it still choked him sometimes. As he wiped away the sweat from his eyes, he looked up and saw Moonie running in the direction of the Cat Cracker. Automatically he knew something was wrong. Nobody ever ran while out in the field, at least not in the direction Moonie was running and not at eleven in the morning. If anybody ran, it was only someone unlucky enough to be still in the field when the whistle blew to signal the day's end – and then he ran toward the gate. He didn't even have his toolbox, so he wasn't headed to work on an emergency job. Eddie started to lock the wrench on another nut, keeping a view of Moonie in the corner of his eye. He slowed to a jog as he got closer to the Cat Cracker. Then he stopped. Eddie could feel his stare. He turned and faced Moonie. Mouth wide open, the aging, overweight man was huffing up a storm. He doesn't even run to the gate at quitting time,

Eddie thought. He gripped his side and bent over for a moment, squinting his eyes, trying to shield himself from sunlight and pain. Then he straightened up a little and waved for Eddie to come to him. Eddie released the pressure in the wrench. Whatever it was that was wrong had something to do with him. He hopped off the platform that held the wrench and half-smiled his way over to Moonie. No one who was watching would know his fear. He slapped Moonie on the back. "What's up, old man?" "Eddie," he said, "there's been a real bad accident at the shop. Malcolm. He's hurt real, real bad. Well, he's not gonna make it. I mean he didn't make it. Malcolm is dead. It just now happened. We don't know how. I just turned around and looked and saw him on the ground. A drill bit some kinda way in his chest. A freak accident." They started to run toward the shop together. "I'm sorry I'm the one to have to tell you. But I just wanted you to find out right away. I mean I figured you'd want to know right away. Dr. Moore is there and it's a ambulance on the way." Moonie stopped running. "You go on," he shouted at Eddie's back.

Eddie heard "Malcolm is dead" over and over again as he ran. Malcolm is dead. And as he ran, he saw his best friend and himself sitting at the bar of their favorite nightclub, The Landing. Just last week. It was Thursday. Ladies' Night. A couple of married men, twenty-seven-year-olds, watching the ladies. Even though Malcolm had been separated from Pam for a while now, Eddie still considered them together. He would always see them together. Somehow the security of his own relationship with Betty depended on Malcolm and Pam still being together. When Eddie thought about their separation, he would see Malcolm and Pam dancing together or laughing or holding hands, and he would hear his own voice, muted, chanting in his head like a Greek chorus: "It's a shame. It's a damned shame. It's a shame. It's a damned shame." He preferred to think of Malcolm the way he was now, sitting here watching the babes. The two of them with wives waiting at home. Yes, he and Malcolm were just two old married men up to no good, the way they should be. They were drinking beer, smoking cigarettes, just a warm-up for later. Eddie had some good smoke in the car. Malcolm didn't usually get high, but he didn't mind if Eddie did. He always talked about how good it smelled. Eddie was saying what he wanted to do to this cute little light-skinned chick standing over by the DJ's booth. Malcolm just nodded and laughed his big happy laugh, like a boy, those lines jutting down from his cheeks and almost meeting at his chin. "Yeah, right," he said. "You're nothin but talk, buddy. Betty would kill you." No, she'd just leave me, Eddie thought beneath his "Nigger, you must be crazy." She had said many times she would and he believed her. (She had ways of making him believe her when she said certain things.) That's why he had to keep secrets, even from Malcolm. He couldn't take the chance of telling even Malcolm. And he felt a real sense of guilt about this, too. It was his obligation to give the details to his buddies. He had shared information with the fellas for as long as he could remember. That was part of the sport as he knew it.

But Malcolm didn't give Eddie the details of his affairs – if, indeed, he had any. (Malcolm had *never* told, though; he was, for reasons Eddie had no inclination to question, exempt from this part of their code. He always had been.) If Malcolm had never been with any woman other than Pam, it would not have surprised Eddie, because Malcolm could be so conservative about certain things. Like not smoking marijuana. And all he ever drank was light beer. If Eddie didn't have marijuana in the car, he'd be drinking Chivas Regal on the rocks. They had already graduated from high school by the time Malcolm started saying the word "fuck" with anything close to conviction. Nope. Maybe he wasn't keeping any secrets from Eddie. Maybe he'd never been to the Chelsea Motel on Hawkins Street in the north end of the city, not four blocks from his own house and Lancaster Park. Maybe Malcolm had never been there at all. Fifteen dollars for four hours. More time than you ever needed. "Nigger, you must be crazy."

"No," said Malcolm. "I'm not crazy and neither is Betty."

"Don't worry about me, chief. I can take care of *my* house –" Eddie tried to stop himself, but it had already slipped out sounding just that way, with ugly implications. Fucking light beer. Not enough real stuff in his system yet to keep him from being clumsy and dangerous. "I didn't mean –" he tried to clean it up. "I didn't mean it like that, Malcolm, you know."

"It ain't no big deal, Eddie," Malcolm said. "Why do you have to make it such a big deal? You don't see me cryin about it." He smiled, a V starting at his chin. "Did you see me cry one day about it?" Eddie just shrugged. "No," Malcolm said. "That's because I never did. There was nothing to cry about. It was just time to go our separate ways."

"Yeah, but shit, man," Eddie started slowly. "I-I-I don't understand. I mean what about the baby? Don't you want to, you know, be around? Watch him grow up and shit?"

"It's not like I left town without telling anybody. I see them all the time. I keep in touch. Hey – I don't brag about it but, you know, I'm really not a bad father. I'm really kinda good to tell you the truth."

Eddie sipped his beer and turned to watch the people out on the dance floor. There was nothing for him to say. He was in no position to give anyone any advice. Malcolm probably was a good father, a better one than Eddie was living in the same house with his children. He took Betty and his kids for granted, he knew. Talking to Malcolm like this might make him go home tonight and tiptoe or stumble into his children's bedroom, still kind of high, and kiss them, but tomorrow or Saturday for sure, he'd be out here again. Home was too restrictive, too small, without enough chances for adventure. Out here was the place to be. Wide open. Out here anything could happen. There was always the chance to catch a high. There were friends, there was booze, there was dope. There were women. They were chances, too; they could be the best highs. There was a hotel he could afford. This was his life. Maybe he would outgrow it someday – and according to Betty he would have to – but right now, he could not resist it. Out here was the place to be. And yet – he couldn't see himself ever giving up Betty the way Malcolm had given up Pam. His life with her was a long way from being hopeless. He needed her. When he was away from her, like now, her restrictiveness became reassuring, like a safety net. And a lot of times, after their arguments, she was a high.

Malcolm tapped him on his shoulder. "Come on. Let's go. I feel like smoking a J."

"You?" Eddie teased. "What is the world coming to?"

They walked outside and stood in front of the club, breathing good air, the music sounding muffled, only the boom-boom of the bass drum filtering out to them. A well-lit corner on the strip. Just hangin' out. All of the chances. And Malcolm chuckling beside him like a boy for no reason, stumbling off the curb as they crossed the street, tipsy off of a couple of light beers, asking for a joint just to make Eddie happy. And, yes, he was happy, because for him, this moment represented the only kind of perfection he knew. He wanted to stand here on this street corner, just helping Malcolm gather his footing and stand up straight, forever.

"Malcolm is dead," Eddie kept hearing as he raced to the shop. As he got closer, he saw the flashing lights, and the siren that had been only an eerie, barely audible musical accompaniment to his thoughts began to register as belonging to an ambulance and not as being a regular plant alarm. He knew that he would not cry no matter how awful it was; he never cried. That was one thing he never had to worry about. If one of them had to be killed here, it was better that it was Malcolm – because if Eddie had been killed, Malcolm would have cried like a baby. You couldn't trust him about things like that. He didn't care enough about what they thought. If Eddie would start bitching to him about something one of them had said to him under his breath or a dirty look one of them had given him, Malcolm would always end up trying to calm him down and say that none of it really mattered. He would start talking about something else. Eddie could tell that he genuinely believed that it didn't really matter. Malcolm had acquired an attitude about a year ago that said nothing on earth really mattered. It wasn't a cynical attitude, however, and, as far as Eddie could tell, it had nothing to do with religion. It was as though he had found the answer to all of his problems. When he and Pam split up, he hadn't missed a beat. The separation seemed to make him happy somehow. He seemed to accept it as part of the plan for his life. That was, it seemed, how he had started to take everything – just as part of the plan for his life. Eddie had yearned for Malcolm to explain it all to him, to tell the source of his ability to look at the world this way. But he knew they never talked about such things; they only put out signals for each other to read. Even Eddie's yearning to know Malcolm's secret was so quiet that he wasn't really aware of the existence of his own desire, which, though only a whisper, amounted to desperation. Still, Eddie had thought that somehow Malcolm would manage to share with him what seemed to be a liberating truth. But no – not now. Malcolm is dead, and he will never be able to reveal to Eddie in some moment filled with one of their silent dialogues what he believed now, while caught in the throes of this tragedy, might have been the key to life, maybe to death, salvation.

But whatever Malcolm's new vision had been, it didn't stop him from crying; Eddie had seen him. At a movie, for Christ's sake. And if Eddie had been lying dead in the shop, Malcolm would definitely have cried, because it didn't matter what they thought. And they would have eaten it up. See the monkey cry. "The only place for a nigger is the zoo with his (pri)mate." That's what the bathroom wall said.

Eddie slowed up as he reached the shop. He could see the paramedics carrying the stretcher because the wheels wouldn't roll on the gravel. Malcolm lay upon it with the metal protruding up from his chest. Eddie walked closer, close enough to touch the body. The paramedics stopped; something about Eddie said they had to. Eddie could feel the eyes upon him. He would not cry. He looked at Malcolm's face and let the blankness he saw there move into the deepest part of himself, shielding his soul from the bombardment of his emotions. From this moment on, even in the most private times, he would never be able to grieve deeply for Malcolm. The paramedics said there was nothing they could do; they were taking him to St. Patrick's. It was the procedure; they were sorry. Then they slid the stretcher into the ambulance, slammed the doors, and drove off. Nobody said anything about Eddie's riding to the hospital, so he figured that doing so must not be the way these things worked. Not part of the procedure. He tried not to think of Malcolm's chest, but it remained fixed in his mind, a shot through the heart, blood soaking through in one massive, dark, wet patch on his old faded green T-shirt. An ugly wound. John Parker, the pipe fitter foreman, came over and told Eddie to come with him to his office; it might be better if he went on home. They walked through the back entrance of the shop. Parker tried to block the puddle from Eddie's view, but it was no use. It was the only spot in the shop that mattered. The flies knew. Eddie stopped. "They're gonna clean it up right away," Parker said. "Jerry!" he yelled too loudly into the unusual silence. "Get Cooper over here to clean this up!" The eyes of the other men nudged Eddie along, and he walked away from the puddle.

Yes, Malcolm is dead, he is thinking, standing with his head down, watching his boots, but about to look up. Dead almost two months. When he looks up he will feel it all, this one time. He will see it all in even greater detail than those who were actually there. Even Moonie had not seen Malcolm fall, but Eddie will. He will see Malcolm fall, and he will see Moonie turning and seeing him lying on the ground. He will see the crowd gather around Malcolm and he will see the eyes accusing R. H. He will see the blood and he will see the flies. He will see it all. And he will hear everything, too. All of the clanging and banging, the metallic buzzing, a scream perhaps. And it will all amount to one sound – the sound of the single shot, Malcolm's, which no one heard: *Pow!*

Now he looks up. Oh, no. Oh, yes. He has seen this all before.

HE IS driving his car on the way home from work, climbing
the I-210 bridge that crosses the lake, grateful to be alone again
after having had Malcolm ride with him for two weeks. That was a
tragedy he does not want to think about. There's just no need for
all that talking while you're crossing the lake. Being alone for this
ride makes matters simpler. The car is rising slowly (rush-hour
traffic has its advantages) up the steep bridge. (The bridge is
steep, but not as steep as the I-10 bridge where the ships that
have business with the port must pass.) Air is rushing in through
the open windows, and Eddie's mouth is open to take some in.
Good air. His ears are popping but, mouth already open, the yawn
is easy. He can just barely hear the radio up here, but he doesn't

need it. Up here he can breathe and think. To the right the water is expanding away. Just a few moments ago he saw three sailboats out there, two coming, one going. The one that was going out started to make a slow turn, an arc – stopped at the 180 degree point, threatened to come back, then completed a circle and continued westward away from the bridge. There were three people on board: two men and one woman, a blond, long legs tanned to gold, hard to tell where they ended and her short, short khaki shorts began. The men were busy guiding the boat, but she lay on her back relaxed, posing for the sun and for Eddie. He noticed the bright orange life jackets and thought how smart the sailors were to be wearing them. (He can't swim.) Diving off the bridge to hitch a ride would be foolish, he had thought looking at the men and the woman; he'd drown. The drowning wouldn't be so bad. It would just be pointless. They weren't even going his way. Thinking about drowning moments ago has him thinking about the beach now. It is over to his left, but he can't see that way because of the blinders placed down the center of the bridge to block the headlights of cars coming from the opposite direction at night. It is because of what happened at the beach that he cannot swim.

His family used to go to the beach all the time. Mama and Daddy, Marcus, his older brother, and Jackie, his little sister. The first time they went that he can remember, the time that it happened, he was five years old. Daddy drove a big beige heap that they jumped into, and then they headed for the beach. It was going to be a picnic because there was food. A large bowl of potato salad was resting in Eddie's lap. Marcus had a pan of seasoned chicken that Daddy would barbecue on one of the pits on the black side of the beach. The side where there were no "Whites Only" signs, the end where the grass was allowed to compete fiercely with the sand for surface space. They parked and Eddie was the first one out of the car, running with the bowl of potato salad to a covered area where there were blue and yellow metal tables and benches. The sand was hot and burned his feet, but it didn't surprise him; this was not his first time here. He couldn't remember the other times, but he had been here before, three or four times maybe. He didn't have to stop and look at the water, wonder at the waves; it was all familiar. He must have been here before. "Edward James Franklin!" his mother yelled. "Boy, if you don't stop all that running." He was laughing, but she could see only his back. Ha. Ha. "Watch out for that bottle glass. And drop that potato salad and I'ma beat your ass." She was always saying she was going to beat his ass for something, and a lot of times she did. Like yesterday when he had said a bad word. Summonabitch! He didn't know what it meant, but Daddy used it all the time. Sometimes he just shouted it at the air when he was angry. Or maybe when he was mad with someone he would use it to talk about them. But sometimes he even used it when he was happy, and it would sort of rumble up out of his chest mixed with laughter. At those times it seemed like such a good word. But even then Eddie knew that "summonabitch" was a bad word. He had said it once too often when Mama was around. She had promised to beat his ass if she ever heard him use it. So when he said it yesterday after he had dropped his last M&M on the kitchen floor, while she was in the same room giving him eyes that were saying you better not pick that up and eat it, and frustration built up in him because with her watching him that way he couldn't even say "God kissed it, the devil missed it" and make it clean, so he couldn't control himself – his last M&M! – couldn't control the way his foot stamped, the way his voice said "Summonabitch!" Yesterday, after that, she rushed over to him like the wind and swatted him on the behind to the rhythm of "What Did I Tell You A-bout Say-ing That Word."

He made it to one of the vacant tables and placed the bowl of potato salad there. The others gathered slowly, his mother carrying two-year-old Jackie, his father with an inflated inner tube he had removed from the trunk of the car, and Marcus carrying the pan of chicken, sulking because Daddy had made him come to the beach with the family. He was old enough to do what he wanted to do. Fifteen! He wanted to stay home and watch TV. When Daddy tried to make him do stuff like this, it really pissed him off. It was just too fuckin hot outside. And that's when Eddie heard the slapping sound coming from the living room, where they were arguing. Daddy's hand meeting some uncovered part of Marcus. Don't ever get pissed off with Daddy, he had told himself, unless you want to get slapped. And if you do get pissed off with him, you better be careful about what you say to him. "Fuckin" was another one of those words like "summonabitch"; you had to be really careful about when you said it. But Eddie wasn't worried about Marcus right now. Right now he was simply happy and glad to be happy. He ran out onto the sand and did a somersault, landing on his ass, but the pain he felt was sweet, because it was *his* tumble and *his* ass, which today had been neither slapped nor beaten.

"Baby, go ahead and start the fire," Daddy said to Mama. "Me and the boys gonna hit the water."

"Jimmy, can't you see I got this child hangin on me? How the hell am I supposed to start a fire?"

"Put her down. She can walk." Jackie smiled at Daddy. "Or give her to me. Daddy gon teach that baby how to swim." He put his arms out to Jackie and she reached for him. But before they could meet, Mama swerved the baby away.

"James, you must be crazy if you think you takin my baby out in that water," she said.

"I'll start the fire, Mama," Marcus broke in.

"That sounds good to me," Daddy said. He smiled at Marcus, who turned away and walked back to the car to get the charcoal.

"Go on then," Mama said to Daddy and Eddie, motioning toward the water.

Eddie, following the line of her outstretched arm, charged across the sand, feeling free. But he could feel that Daddy was chasing him. The ground quaked beneath his feet from Daddy's heavy trodding. The trembling surface seemed to jump up and

meet Eddie's steps halfway, while his knees were still bent, putting an extra strain on the muscles in his little-boy legs, and somehow tickling his stomach, so that he had slowed to a creeping
hunched-over walk and was overcome with wild laughter by the
time Daddy came up behind him and swooped him up and onto a
solid shoulder. It was one of Eddie's favorite spots to sit and he
reveled in being placed there now. Daddy was carrying the inflated inner tube on his other shoulder, and Eddie slapped at it
with the hand that wasn't gripped around Daddy's neck. Rising
up to meet Eddie's nose was Daddy's huffing breath, hot and
sweet as it usually was. It was the same hot sweetness that kissed
him late at night sometimes while he was dreaming. ("Leave him
alone. You gonna wake him up, you drunken fool.") He bobbed up
and down on Daddy's shoulder, the water getting closer. Then
Daddy splashed in and began to slow down quickly as the water
rose to his knees. They continued to move ahead and when the
water came up to Daddy's waist, he let the inner tube fall from his
shoulder and rest upon the water. He placed Eddie on the inner
tube and told him to hold on. The water was cool on Eddie's legs as
they dangled in the water through the empty middle of the inner
tube. Daddy began pushing Eddie out farther into the lake. He
looked at Daddy's hand, so big, on the inner tube next to his; he
looked across the expansive lake, tiny green-black waves washing
toward him; his head fell back, and there was the sky – way, way
up. Floating along, he closed his eyes. Everything was so big, so
much bigger than he was. You might as well surrender to these
forces. A good feeling, being carried. Like when you fell asleep
sometimes while watching television in the living room and they
came in and tried to wake you up to go get into your bed, but you
pretended to be still asleep. They had to pick you up and carry you
down the hall to your room, for a second, their eyes all over your
face. They were gonna beat your ass if you were faking, but you
knew that wasn't true because they kissed you on the neck and

laid you on the bed gently, pulled up the covers, and kissed you again.

Now Daddy stopped pushing. Eddie opened his eyes, looked back, and saw that the sand was far away. He could barely see Mama, Marcus, and the baby under the covering. The wind turned the inner tube slowly, and he watched as Daddy disappeared underwater with a slurping sound. He was out of sight so long that Eddie began to wonder if he would come back. ("Is he coming back, Mama?" "Yes, baby. Now go on back to bed." "Me, I don't care if he never come back. Always drunk and carrying on. Hmph – tryin to tell me what to do." "Marcus, shut up before I have to hit you." "I guess you have to hit somebody. . . . " "What did you say?" "Nothing." "Don't cry, Mama. Daddy comin back.") Then Daddy whooshed up through the inner tube, filling up the middle with his body and flying water. Eddie felt the big hands locking in his armpits and he kicked his legs in pleasure as he rose high above Daddy's head. "Put me down, put me down," he cried, wanting never to come down. But Daddy did let him down, placed him safely on the floating tube. Then Daddy swam around while Eddie splashed water with his hands. The dark green color of the water intrigued him, so he cupped some in his hands and brought it to his face. It smelled fresh. He stuck out his tongue and dipped it in the water. Salt. The water had a flavor. Clear water tasted like nothing. Green water tasted like salt. Tasting it made him hungry. Watching Daddy swimming and splashing in it made him hungry.

Then Daddy went under again. Eddie watched for him intensely. Where did Daddy go? He wanted to know. Why and how did he always come back? He wanted to know, but he felt powerless. He didn't know how he would ever be able to find out the answers to his questions. But maybe if he could get under the water to follow Daddy, he would have a chance to answer them. It couldn't be very hard to do, going under. It looked so easy, the way

Daddy splashed around, going under and coming up as he pleased. But Daddy was big, like the lake; he was too little. How would he ever be able to get under the water to follow Daddy? In frustration he slapped at the surface of the water. Then he kicked at it as hard as he could, but it wouldn't let his legs move through it very fast. It pushed hard back against them. It was a force. He was too little; it was so big. It was a force. He would surrender to it. But since it already knew he was a fighter, he would have to trick it. Pretend to be asleep. It would believe him. They wanted to believe you; they liked to carry you. He pushed himself from his seat on the tube, then let his body go limp. Sliding downward through the middle of the tube, he felt the water hug around him coolly. It was carrying him down, it covered his head, it began to cool his insides, entering through his mouth and through his nose and through his ears. There was a salty burning that soon went quiet. The water flooded his head with waves that washed away Daddy first and then everything else. Then it closed above him in a kiss. Below the surface, it kept carrying him away.

*   *   *

"LORD, have mercy," Mama was saying in a scared, low voice. "The man done killed his own child."

"Shut up, Dorothy," Daddy said, almost directly into Eddie's ear. He was close. "The boy is all right. Don't come running over here with none of your foolishness. I don't wanna hear that shit, woman."

Eddie was struggling to open his eyes.

"Oh, yeah, you gon hear it, all right. You ain't gon kill my child and git away with it."

"Woman, the boy is breathing. Look at here – he just opened up his eyes."

Eddie saw Daddy's face up close, the red eyes that had a wet, sunny sparkle of happiness in them holding his attention. "You all right, Eddie," Daddy assured him in hot sweetness. "You all right, son."

"Well, don't just keep him out here in this hot sun, James. Let's git him in the shade," Mama was saying. "Maybe he need to go to the hospital." Daddy picked Eddie up in his arms, cradling him, and walked toward the covering.

"Daddy, I don't want to know how to swim," Eddie coughed out. Daddy nodded his head okay, okay; he understood. But Eddie would get over it. This was just one bad experience. He wouldn't be afraid of the water forever. Someday he'd want to learn how to swim, and Daddy would teach him. But then that meant that he really did not understand Eddie at all. Eddie wasn't afraid of the water. He meant that he really *didn't* want to know how to swim. Not because he was afraid of the water, but because the drowning was okay. The water could carry you to a good place. He didn't want to learn how to swim, because if he did, he'd be forced to do what Daddy did: keep coming back.

The beach is special; he will have to remember to bring Tammy and Edward Junior there more often. He has to pick them up from the day-care center on his way home. It's just a block away after he gets off at the second exit on the other side of the bridge. About two and a half miles away. Tammy in the sandbox, Edward Junior on the merry-go-round. Eddie likes to drive up and see them playing. Tammy will look up, see his car coming, and clap her hands. The ribbons in her hair will be drooping from her hard day's work. Her hair won't grow, so Betty puts in all those ribbons. They look pretty, though. Just like the tiny gold earrings. Pretty. Edward Junior will not be ready to leave. He'll want to stay on the merry-go-round. Eddie remembers liking the merry-go-round, too, as a boy. (Maybe his son will grow up to be just like him.) He will be kind and gently pluck him from the spinning ride. They will all ride home together, the kids teaching him the alphabet, the colors, how to count to ten or a hundred. He loves this. He can't wait to get over this bridge.

:02

AND HE WAS 24 YEARS OLD...

HE IS scratching his head nonchalantly with two fingers, and he is thinking: I am —

You can lay there on that couch and act like you don't hear me if you want to – but I'm telling you, the next time I find that stuff in this house, I'm flushing it down the toilet. I don't care how much it's worth. And from the size of that bag, there must have been a hel-luva lot in there. I can't guess what it must have cost you, but it probably would have been enough to keep them people from calling me on my job and upsetting my nerves about the bill for that couch you're laying there relaxing on. As much money as we make be-tween us, there's no reason why we can't make ends meet. If I can

47

bring all of mine home, you can, too. After we get the bills paid, you can have the rest to have your fun with. I'm not even gon try to tell you that you can't smoke whatever you want, because you gon do what you want to do anyway. And I know you gon go out sometimes and come home drunk because you just like your daddy. I can't do nothing about that and I don't even know if you can. But, hell, how about a little effort, you know? Because there's a limit to how much I can take. There's a limit.

You don't know how I felt when I walked into that bedroom and saw that child standing in the middle of the floor with that bag in his hand, digging in it like it was a bag of candy. I thought I was dreaming. I kept saying, This is a dream. I don't believe this. This is a dream. But it wasn't a dream because I could smell it. It was real and I knew whose fault it was. That's one thing right there, Eddie. The children. If I have to teach you how to show respect for them, then there really is no hope. But I think you know better. You're not crazy. Just careless. You forgot that your children like to crawl around on closet floors and dig in shoe boxes and things. You forgot that this time. I can understand that this one time. But I don't think I could understand it again. You're gonna have to remember them next time. Because if it happens again, I hate to think about what's going to happen to us. I know the first thing I'd do is flush the stuff down the toilet. But I don't know what would happen after that. I know this much – there wouldn't be any questions asked. No chance for explanations. Not that you ever explain anything anyway. But, really, what could you say? It would only be twice as awful as it is right now. So I wouldn't say anything. Just flush. And after that... well, who knows – I might be on my way. That's not a threat, really. Just a prediction. I wouldn't have any control over myself. This is who I am. Am I being a bitch about this? Am I asking too much of you? I don't think so.

Goodness, Eddie. Do you think the kids don't know when you've been out there gettin high and carrying on? Do you think they don't care? Well, Tammy, maybe she doesn't. She's too young to *know any better. But not Edward Junior. You should see the way he runs to his bedroom when he hears your car pull up in the driveway late on a Friday or Saturday night. He'll be in here rolling around a truck or something, and I woulda been telling him all night how it's time for him to go to bed and he'd keep saying how he's not sleepy – and then you turn into the driveway and he runs to the back and crawls into bed. He's not afraid of you. You know that. He just doesn't want to see the way you and me don't look at one another when you walk in the front door. He doesn't want any part of it. Just four years old. But I can't blame him. A lot of times I don't want any part of it either, and I run to the back with him and crawl into bed myself. And then you come in here smellin up the whole house, stumbling over a toy truck or train or something and talkin real loud. You be thinkin you talking in a whisper, but you be real loud. And every time that happens, I just lay in bed telling myself that that's the last time it'll happen, that you'll never do it again. Sometimes I can really make myself believe it.*

You know, I know you could be a whole lot worse. I've seen worse. My daddy was a whole lot worse. Your daddy is a whole lot worse, too. I hear you in here telling your stories about your daddy to Malcolm and them. I hear you in here just a-laughing at what a scandal your daddy was. I've heard you tell many a time the story about the time your daddy had some woman in the bed at your house. In your mama's house, Eddie. And you just a-laughing while you tell that story, Eddie. And about how you had to help him sneak that woman out of the house because you saw your mama coming down the street. You just laugh when you tell that one. When you tell that one and all those other stories about your daddy and all of his women. You and all the rest of your friends laugh at that stuff, Eddie. Malcolm, too. He doesn't laugh as hard as you think he laughs – but he still laughs. And you – you laugh the hardest, Eddie. Way too hard. Harder than anybody else. You like that kinda stuff too much. I think you wish you could be like your daddy. But you have to be better than him. Because you know that's something I won't stand for. I always let you know that, Eddie. I couldn't take you messing around with other women. When you married me, you said good-bye to all of that. You said I was all you wanted and needed and I believed you. When the day comes that you decide you need more than me, that's the day I decide I need better than you. That's something I'm not about to put up with. You could go out there, mess with the wrong woman, and come back and give me VD. I know that happens because my own daddy did that. Went out and messed around and came back home and gave my mama syphilis. Twice. You hear me? You remember – I told you about that late one night. I remember. I was about four or five years old, and I had to go to the clinic with her when she went to get her shots. I was too young to know what was going on then, but I figured it out later and made Mama tell me. She didn't want me to know. She thought I would hold it against my daddy. And I guess I did. I still do. I'm just glad she had the courage and good sense to let him go. I take after my mama, Eddie. I may not be a courageous woman, but I do have good sense. And if I ever find out about you and another woman, I'm pretty sure I could let you go. Again, that's a prediction. I'll never forget that clinic.

I know you don't want to hear all of this. But I think it's important. Sometimes we have to talk about stuff like this – no matter how uncomfortable it makes us feel. Otherwise, it'll all be over and we'll never even know what happened to us. I'm just saying that I want everything clear between us. I don't want there to be any misunderstandings. I think it only makes sense to let you know exactly what it is I expect from you. Talking about it this way might be the only way to keep anything bad from ever happening.

I was just thinking. I don't know how your mama does it. I don't know how she takes all of that from your daddy. All those women. The illegitimate children. And all the rest of what he does. I think you know that if you ever raise your hand to hit me the way he does your mama, you've seen the last of me. Strong prediction. God, I don't know how Dorothy takes all that from him. I can understand loving the man – but not that much. Love can make people do crazy things, I guess. But taking a beating is way past crazy. I could never do that. I'd rather lie in my bed alone every night and cry myself to sleep. I'd rather have a broken heart than a broken neck any day.

You must know what that kinda stuff does to children. You must know. You grew up with it. You must remember how that was. I remember my Aunt Connie. Me and Coco used to go over to her house and spend the night with our cousins Janet and Roxanne all the time. Uncle Herbert musta been crazy, the way he beat her sometimes. And you never knew when it was gonna happen. Sometimes he wouldn't be drinkin or anything. He might be sitting in the living room in his old beat-up green leather chair calmly watching TV, and then the next thing you knew, all hell had broke loose. I remember how we would already be in bed sometimes and then suddenly there was all this screamin. Aunt Connie would be yelling at the top of her lungs, "Help me! Lordy! Help me! He's gon kill me!" You could hear the licks, the way he was slapping her. Why doesn't she kill him, I used to wonder. Pick something up and kill him. And then I would wonder why she was still in that house, as many times as he put her through that, as many beatings as he gave her. It used to make my stomach hurt to lay there and listen to her screamin. A lump in my throat so big I couldn't even swallow. And Janet and Roxanne would lay in bed and not move. But you knew they were crying because you could hear the sniffling. And if you said something to them, they'd just act like they were sleeping. And in the morning they wouldn't even look at you. They always said they were tired and wanted to sleep late. Scared to get up and look at you. Too ashamed. Ashamed of their daddy for all of his craziness and ashamed of their mama for being so weak. And when we finally did get up we would see Aunt Connie's face all beat up. I couldn't even eat my breakfast. And we had already missed the car-

toons because we had slept so late. That musta happened I don't know how many times when we went over there to spend the night. Finally we just stopped asking to go.

Poor Aunt Connie. The way some of the women in the family used to talk about her. Johnnie Mae was the worst. She would sit her fat self on Mama Sally's porch and just go on and on about how bad Aunt Connie looked. I can hear her now. "Girl, you seen Connie lately? Honey, she is truly a mess. That man done whipped her ass again. Sho as I tell you. She got this knot on her jaw that's all kinds of colors. And you know she ain't no pretty woman to start with. Plus all them scars and things. But Herbert has truly whipped her ass this time. One of the worse I ever seen. And, girl, you know I done seen many of the beatins Herbert has put on her. But this is one of the worse. Connie just can't control him. Been beatin her silly since the wedding day. But I tell you somethin. For all those beatins, that girl has still got that figure. Ain't she? Connie always did *have a figure." That's what it all came down to – Aunt Connie had a figure and she didn't. Johnnie Mae was just jealous – the fat cow. They all did their share of talking about her. But if she woulda left Uncle Herbert they woulda talked about her even more, like they talked about my mama the first time she mentioned leaving my daddy. They said she was breaking up the family. Leavin those children without a daddy. They didn't care how scary no goddamn clinic was, they said. You better stay with that man. They woulda told Aunt Connie the same thing if she had tried to leave Uncle Herbert. And she woulda listened to them, too. But she knew better than to even talk about leaving him. She knew she wasn't strong enough to take what they would say about her just for bringing it up. She wasn't strong enough, even if she did have a good figure. She couldn't have put them in their place the way Mama did. She couldn't have told Johnnie Mae that she was a fat cow and that she should wait until she found a man and kept him for more than a month before she started talking about other people. Aunt Connie couldn't have told Aunt Barbara how low she was to sit out on her mama's back porch and listen to all that crap about her own sister without standing up for her. And she couldn't have told Mama Sally that she was the worst one of them all for letting them use her porch like that. She couldn't have told her own mama that she was the worst of them all. But that's the way Mama told them. Put all of them in their place. And she never heard a peep out of them after that. When she finally left my daddy, none of them said a word to her. She wasn't like her sister. She wasn't like your mama. She was a different kind of woman. And so am I.*

In some ways I'm even more demanding. So I'm insisting that you demand more of yourself than your daddy did of himself. And then – then maybe Edward Junior might demand more of himself. You know, and so on. And then maybe one day no black woman will have to play this same old, tired song again. It's starting to drag, like a record being played at the wrong speed.

You know, and maybe no woman will have to use a pot of grits the way you made me do that morning. I know you remember those grits. I didn't know what I was doing, really. It was maybe even going to be a joke. Before I did it I thought, Well, if he laughs, I'll laugh, too. But you didn't laugh. You just froze, afraid, guilty. That look on your face gave you away. I was crushed by your reaction. It just proved to me what I had suspected the night before. Something in the way you handled me. So arrogant. So possessive, like you owned me. It's hard to explain. I don't know the words. But I do know that when I fixed those grits I wanted you to know that even though I was yours, I was still mine. *You know what I mean. I thought maybe we could see that together without saying anything and laugh about it some kinda way. But then – that look on your face. And I thought, This son of a bitch is guilty. I was hurt, so I let you think I was a bitch. Because I thought you deserved that. You deserved to have to put up with a bitch. And now, right this minute, you ain't listening to me. I'm trying to tell you I'm sorry about that. I'm sorry that I couldn't laugh it off back then. I was so young. We both were. I was trying to figure out who I was going to be. I*

53

couldn't have you deciding that for me. But now I realize that re-
gardless of who I am to myself, in your mind I can only be who you
want me to be. It doesn't really matter what I think. You know what
I mean? And when you look at it that way, it really is kinda funny,
you know. I guess I'm just saying that I can be yours because I
know I'm really mine. That's funny. I can laugh about it now. You
could too, except you're not listening to me. If you were you would
be over here in a flash, all over me, thinking it's make-up time already. I know you. And I could deal with that. But you're not listening, and that's okay, too—because I'm not so sure that I want to
reveal this much of myself to you today. I am angry.

   You probably think I just love doing this, talking like this. But I
don't. I hate it. I don't get no kinda thrill from standing up here
making background music for your daydreams and fantasies. I
can tell you let most of what I say go in one ear and out the other,
but I hope that you hear some of what I'm saying, because it's scary
to think about our future otherwise. There won't be any stopping
the worse from happening if you go too far. Not a threat, a prediction. The world keeps turning, and neither one of us can stop it. I
won't be able to control my reactions. I am who I am. You hear me?
Well . . . anyway, that's all I have to say. I might make a point of
repeating myself from time to time, but I've said it all just now. If
something bad happens, it won't be because I didn't try to tell you
what I expected from you. I have spoken my piece.

– uncomfortable.

AND HE WAS 28 YEARS OLD...

HE IS standing at the window of his bedroom looking out at his neighbors, Debra and Mark. A car has just driven into their driveway and they are helping their guests move boxes, luggage, and children from the car into the house. Seeing the car next door and not in his own driveway has calmed Eddie. When he heard the car pull up a few moments ago he jumped from the bed, afraid that it might have been Betty coming home for some reason. He convinced himself even before he made it to the window that it couldn't possibly be Betty, that she was safely out of the scene, miles away with the kids in Galveston for a family reunion with her side of the family. But he thought it might be someone they knew. That was possible. So he didn't really stop panicking until he had seen for certain that the car was next door.

He believes the people he sees Debra and Mark helping into the house are Debra's sister and brother-in-law. Debra is in a robe and slippers and she is carrying a sleeping little girl, her niece. Mark is lugging a couple of suitcases. The sister looks frantic and confused – half of her head in curlers, the other half in rebellion – just standing by the front door to the house, leaning against the mailbox, clutching her purse. Her husband is carrying a large, heavy box that is catching some of the ashes from the cigarette dangling between his lips. There seems to be some whispering going on among them, though no one is speaking. Something somber, but Eddie's not quite sure what's going on. Refugees, he thinks – without knowing why. Somehow the word seems to fit, though he cannot really say what it means. Underground Railroad, he thinks, again not knowing why – though he knows exactly what that means. Is there some kind of escape going on? Maybe that's it. Or. . . or maybe the connection he is making has to do with the stars he sees above (far in the background) in the clear night sky, maybe with the moon, which is not even placed within the frame of his bedroom window. Maybe that's the connection. The Underground Railroad: They had to travel on clear nights to make full use of the stars. He sees drawings in an old library book he read, really read, in the seventh or eighth grade – one of the few books he has ever read from beginning to end. The drawings, he remembers, showed runaway slaves in various stages along the Underground Railroad. Sneaking through the woods and looking up at the stars. Showing white men phoney traveling papers. Work-muscled black bodies squeezing into small crates to hide, so that they could be smuggled. Quakers, strange white people. And Harriet Tubman, not a sketch or simple drawing, but a real portrait. She was a tough-looking black woman whose face told you that she didn't take much shit. Eddie can never remember the complete title of the book, but he knows that the word "freedom" was in it. And he remembers the book as that: *Freedom*. A dusty old book with pages turning yellow on the way to brown. After reading it, he started checking out books all the time, but rarely did he get around to reading them. One or two he read, but *Freedom* was the only book he had any memory of. Looking out his bedroom window at the almost furtive poses of his neighbors and their relatives, he thinks there must be all kinds of Underground Railroads, all kinds of refugees, and all kinds of freedom.

He is totally naked as he stands at the window. His penis is extending away from his body and lightly touching the cool wall. He feels her eyes looking at his back, as his buttocks tighten and his scrotum creeps. The tiny imperceptible hairs on his back have risen and are doing a dance of stiff motion, as if being rustled by a breeze. Cathy is her name and she is about to ask him what he's doing out of bed. That's what she's going to say. "What are you doing out of bed, Eddie?" And with the mingling of the calmness he feels from knowing that the car is next door and the excitement he's overcome with from the utter sexuality of this moment, guilt suddenly appears, like precipitation from some chemical reaction.

But he'd felt no guilt before. When Betty reminded him about the family reunion a week ago, the idea to bring Cathy here formed instantly in his mind. He was quick to pretend that he'd completely forgotten about the reunion. Told her he had agreed to work some weekend overtime at the plant. She was disappointed at first, but she didn't protest very strongly. After all, there was really nothing wrong with a man making a little extra money when he could. She and the kids would ride down to Galveston with her mother. No problem. Then this afternoon: There were leftover pork chops and cabbage in the refrigerator, all you had to do was heat it up, cook a pot of rice in the rice cooker, try not to make a mess. She'd call tomorrow morning and wake him up for work. She loved him, God help her.

God help her. If she'd only known what he was up to.

In bringing Cathy here, to this house, to Betty's house, Eddie is shit, he knows. That's why he starts to panic with every car he hears passing on the street. Guilt and fear. But he has to have Cathy. He just has to. And his house, vacant for the weekend, is ideal. When he had suggested to Cathy that the two of them get together at his house, she didn't hesitate in agreeing to coming over for the night. She knew the alternatives: her apartment, which he hates, and the Chelsea Motel, which she says makes her feel like a slut.

Her apartment depresses him. It isn't really an apartment at all; it's half of a crumbling old duplex in the middle of the city, a few blocks north of Q. D. Jacob High, where Eddie went to high school, not more than three blocks from where he grew up on Pine Street. He likes the way he feels when he drives in the vicinity of his old neighborhood, when he and Cathy choose to spend the night or part of the night together at her place. The way they slide out of the club and walk across the discreet back parking lot to his car. They fire up a joint in the car and they're off on the slow ride to her place. A left on the strip, then a right at the first light onto Hampton Street, which leads to his old neighborhood. On Hampton they travel two long blocks, passing Jack's Liquor Store on the right, a blinking neon Budweiser sign in the window, brothers swinging out of Jack's glass doors clutching bottle-shaped brown paper bags. The second long block ends with the railroad tracks. A left on State Street running along the east side of the tracks, then the "tree" streets start intersecting State. Cathy's street is first, Cypress. He passes it; he wants to finish off the joint first. Willow Street follows, then Oak, where Malcolm grew up. So the next street has to be Pine. His old street. He makes a right. There, in the middle of the block, that's where he used to live. She knows the people who live there now. There must be about ten children. Damn, only three bedrooms, he says; she knows. He likes the way this feels. This driving and watching, remembering and telling. But when he turns right on Sutton Street to go back down to Cypress, he begins to feel the discomfort. Her old duplex imposes itself on him as soon as he rounds the corner. A street light is placed across the street from it, so light floods out over it, showing vividly the once-white building, the peeling paint. He sees the two rusting screen doors, both ajar (always ajar, something fundamentally wrong at the hinges) at opposite ends of the wide front porch, to which you climb up on cracking concrete steps. He hates it. It's ugly. He knows ugly when he sees it, and this is ugly. But it's also all she can afford. A cashier at A&P, and inside her half of the duplex, two young boys. They sometimes make him feel even worse than the outside of her place does. Indeed, if he didn't have to deal with the possibility of seeing the kids, the looks of the place probably wouldn't disgust him so.

The youngest boy is the real problem. Eddie cannot even remember his name, if Cathy ever even mentioned it to him. But the first time he walked through the front door to the apartment with Cathy, the little boy turned from the television, jumped up, and ran over to him with a big smile on his face. "Daddy!" he yelled at Eddie with his arms stretched out, expecting Eddie to pick him up. "Daddy!" Eddie was taken by surprise and almost instinctively picked up the boy as his own. But he hesitated, and Cathy picked up the child and whisked him away to a back bedroom. When she came back into the living room, their conversation started quickly and they never said a word about the incident. Eddie remembers the little boy and wonders who his father is. He wonders if the kid ever sees his real father. He must have seen him at least once because he expects to see him again. He wonders how many others like him walk through the front door and disappoint the boy. Will he ever see his father again? The ugly outside of the duplex gives Eddie little reason to hope that he will.

Cathy's objections to the Chelsea Motel are as strong as Eddie's are to her place. Nothing but prostitutes and fags go there, she says. Does he think of her as just another slut? The one time they went there, she made him get out of the car first and open the door to the room. Then she made a quick dash inside. She checked the lock behind her and stood at the door observing the place. Eddie threw his keys on the end table and flopped down on the bed, which took up practically all of the space in the room. There was only about a two-foot-wide path of indoor-outdoor carpeting surrounding it. Standing at the door, she was too good-looking for the place. Eddie had to admit it to himself. The light directly above her head was slicing away at her pretty face. She tapped the door at her right, and a piercing squeak showed her the barely usable bathroom. She winced. "Don't think about it," he told her. "Think about me." Slapping a place beside him on the bed, he said, "Come on and sit down." She shifted her feet, her red heels catching the light, her firm jean-wrapped thighs lightly grazing one another. "Come on." Then she stepped out from under the light and her face came back together beautifully. Only two steps and he had her by the waist with both hands and was pulling her down into his lap. "It ain't so bad," he whispered in her ear. "Besides – once we get started, you ain't gon know where you at anyway." They laughed and rolled over and lay on the bed embracing. But their lovemaking was not nearly as fulfilling as it usually was for Eddie. Cathy didn't seem to let go the way she did at other times. And when they finished, she couldn't keep still in his arms and finally asked him to take her home.

So he and Cathy are at his house. It is here or no place at all. And there's no question that they have made the right decision, the way they have already made love tonight. When they are at their best, this is how they make love: Smoothing hair away from her creamy brown forehead, his fingers trace their way down to an ear. She raises her shoulder in defense. "No, that tickles," she says with a half-laugh. She has large round eyes, dark brown, and long lashes that guard them. Her lips are thick, a darker brown than the caramel face; they are now whipped clean by his own and are glowing. They entice him and he kisses her. His eyes close automatically and he marvels at how quickly his heaviness becomes hard. Impatient, she grabs him by the elbow and pulls him on top of her. This is the way she is, the way he is, when it is right. They can't seem to get enough of each other. The way she grabs everything she wants. (She bites her nails – no need for caution or undeserved kindness.) Fuck me, she says. All night, he answers. All night. His arms are wrapped under her back and his hands come up and grip her soft, round shoulders. She embeds her fingers in the low forest of his hair and presses his mouth hard on her breasts, so soft they seem to give way to the shape of his face like a liquid. He manages to lift his head a little, touches his tongue to a nipple. Fleshy, but hard and perfectly round like the pearl of an oyster. She presses his head down even harder; it is good. No matter how violently he moves his head, she does not let him up for air. He keeps raising and lowering his body at the hips to meet her rhythm. Amazing, the way she is pulling him into her, how far she is pulling him into her. Keep this rhythm, he tells himself. Keep her rhythm and she will let you know all of her secrets. Keep this rhythm, keep this rhythm. She will let you know how deep she is, how far and wide. She will let you know what goes on beneath her, what is at the bottom, what is on the other side. He is sinking and rising at the same time, faster and faster, until the two motions are canceling each other, and he finds himself suspended in a vacuum.

This is how they make love. And as shitty as he feels, he will not be denied this pleasure. All he has to do is think about it, how good it is, and the guilt that could be so overwhelming is almost nonexistent. He cannot understand it, but he senses that somewhere within him there is something, some little, tiny something that will prove his innocence. Maybe not to anyone other than himself, but that would be enough. If he can ever get to this place and touch, feel, *see* this thing, he will know that he is not shit, really, but that he is good. It is the mere promise of this that gives him the strength to find pleasure in this night. So when Cathy calls him back to the bed, when she says to him, "What are you doing out of bed Eddie?" he will turn and walk toward her, out of the starlight, into her arms, under a halo of guilt.

: 0 3

AND HE WAS 29 YEARS OLD...

HE IS walking out of his house through the back door, which opens to his freshly cut backyard. Odd, this swift crisp smell of the grass that is so reminiscent of winter, but which he knows only comes during these warmer days. It is blended with the sweet smell of the ham bone in his hand that he is going to take to the back fence and toss over to Princess, the collie who lives in the adjoining backyard, and with the insistent odor from the glass of scotch in his other hand. Vapors from the scotch are insinuating themselves through his nasal passages and then lapping at the back of his throat. There is breeze enough to fly a kite, but it's not the season. He hears the leaves blowing in the cypress trees and his mind shifts to September and October, the time when they will fall and he will have to rake them and stuff them into black-green plastic bags. But a wasp *zzzes* past his ear and it is August again.

His eyes follow the yellow path kids have made along the left side of Princess's house, and he sees beyond the houses on the distant street to the horizon where the sun is going down. The clouds there are fluffy, painstakingly designed, and bright, bright orange, like something in one of Tammy's coloring books. Even God must use Crayola. He sees the hand of God, itself made of cloud-stuff, with long slender fingers and with a wrist that fades into and out of invisibility, reaching into the green and yellow box, going straight for the orange, lifting it by the tip and sliding it out delicately to leave the paper covering behind. God's hand holds the crayon, not with the point against the sky but with the long, smooth side flat against it, and shades in blank clouds against a horizon somewhere in the universe, all fingers on the crayon except the pinky, which is raised. Dainty, God. And yet somewhere out there attached to the hand there is a forceful man-like something that falls into the category of the strong, silent type.

His backyard registers as a neat green square that connects to other green squares. These will eventually lead to slabs of con-crete, which accumulate to form a road. The road extends to the edge of a body of water; the water, in the distance, washes up against the wall of blue, the sky, which domes over mankind. At this moment it is so pleasing to think of the world in this way that he finds it hard to believe anyone ever thought it necessary to question the earth's flatness.

Backyards. Where you find children, trees, and pets. Barbe-cues. He remembers the only backyards other than this one that he has known intimately: the backyard behind the old house he grew up in on Pine Street and the one that bordered his own, Mal-colm's. A line dividing the two yards was drawn by a straight row of five trees, two pines on each side of an oak. The trees stood like

candles in a birthday cake with thick green icing, and as young
boys Eddie and Malcolm, thinking that it might actually be sweet,
chewed a few blades of grass, only to spit them out quickly along
with several wads of contaminated saliva, their mouths rejecting
the bitter taste. A path led from the back door of each boy's house
to the oak tree, their favorite meeting place. Beneath the oak they
would tell each other all of the new things they had learned about
the world. They would teach each other new things there beneath
the oak. There Eddie told Malcolm that there was no such thing
as Santa Claus, and there Malcolm showed Eddie how four quar-
ters equal one dollar. Eddie showed Malcolm how to play marbles,
and Malcolm showed Eddie the right way to write a capital E.
(They were writing their names in a dirt spot with twigs when
Malcolm noticed that the first letter of his friend's name was written backward. "That's not how you make a E," he told Eddie.
"Watch me. First you draw a long line straight down, like this.
Then you make a long line *thisaway.* Then you make a short line
thisaway. Then you make another long line *thisaway.* Then you
got a E.") Eddie can't remember the first time he and Malcolm
met and played in the backyards; it just seems that one day, there
they were—not beneath the oak, but up in its highest branches
discussing the art of flying. As Eddie recalls it, they must have
been about six years old, somewhere around the time they started
to go to Washington Elementary, and the final consensus was
that if they were birds, they would be able to fly. ("If we was a bird
we could fly.") Interestingly, it also seems to Eddie that the last
time they climbed the tree together they also talked about flying,
only by this time Malcolm had discovered, in one of the many
books he was always reading, that there were stories about people
who could really fly. Africans, he told Eddie, who didn't believe it
for a second. They were thirteen at the time, too old for such shit.
No one, Eddie said, could fly. People were not birds. Then Malcolm began to tell Eddie about how he would sometimes lie beneath this very tree in which they were now perched, close his

eyes, and gradually feel his body levitate. His head and chest would slowly rise upward, bringing him into a vertical position, and his feet would dangle just above the ground. He felt like a helium balloon. A force pushed up into his armpits, and he couldn't bring his arms down to his sides. The force gave him a thick, satisfying dizziness that reminded him of the way he felt when he smelled bread baking. It had something to do with heat. Not with burning, but with warmth. His seriousness frightened Eddie. Malcolm was smarter than he was, he knew, far too smart to be so passionate about something as ridiculous as his being able to fly – even if it was only in his dreams. And now Malcolm was going on to say he realized that it was only a daydream, but it felt so real. And it was something that he could make happen whenever he wanted it to. All he had to do was lie down underneath the oak. And did Eddie know what it was a lot like? It was a lot like when they came out in the middle of the night sometimes and, without saying more than three words to each other, sat back-to-back, feet propped against ground-breaking roots for leverage, and stroked themselves at the groin, arms flailing at the elbows, bringing themselves to climaxes. (Eddie cringed; they had made a silent but solemn promise never to mention this. He regarded Malcolm with a look of malice that, before he could stop it, had turned traitor and become filled with awe and admiration; there was an undeniable bravery in his having the courage to speak it, and an equally undeniable superiority in his having spoken it first.) It was a lot like that in that he could make it happen anytime he wanted to and in that it felt so good. But it happened at night, too, while he was sleeping, when he had no control over it. Like a wet dream. He would wake up sometimes, spent from flight (at night he would soar), confused about exactly where he was – in his bed, under the oak, or in the Sunbeam Bread factory they had taken a tour through in the fourth grade. He knew it wasn't real, but now there was this book he had lucked up on. He hadn't told anybody else about his dreams, he said. Eddie told him to keep it that way.

People already thought Malcolm was weird enough as it was, a self-confessed virgin and everything. All they needed was something like this to confirm his lunacy.

It was Malcolm who introduced Eddie to the word "virgin." Eddie already knew the implications of being someone who had "never had no pussy" – primarily because he was one of those people – but he did not know the word itself. Malcolm defined the word and admitted to being one practically in the same breath. To Eddie such an admission was unbelievable. He had learned early on (it was a part of him) that innocence was an affliction from which only the less fortunate, the less manly, suffered. About eleven at the time, Eddie had fabricated a lie about his having "done it" for the first time long ago. He said he was eight years old when he and Tanya McClain, the girl who had just moved from California, had sneaked off into the alley behind Hanchey's Drugstore one day. They hid in a big cardboard box and he got on top of her. He raised up her dress and saw that she didn't have on any underwear. His hand went right to the spot. She tried to stop him, but it was too late. He unbuttoned his pants and made her do it. After a while she started to like it. That was a long time ago, and he had done it a lot of times since then; he wasn't a virgin. He had had pussy before. (Part of his story had really happened. He and Tanya had hidden in a box behind Hanchey's Drugstore when he was eight. It was part of a game of hide-and-seek. They had wandered off together and found themselves huddled closely in this dark place. No one would ever find them here. They were safe. So close, they kissed; it was natural. The kiss made Eddie dizzy. His heart began to beat loudly. Could she hear it? How could she *not* hear it! How embarrassing! She must have thought he was such a baby. He'd have bet anything that boys in California didn't have hearts that beat with stupid fear the way his was doing. California was another world. They probably had hearts that barely beat at all. But maybe she didn't mind his inexperience, because now she was brushing her lips across his again. So close. They were

69

doing it. They were doing *it.*) Many of the other boys had stories as well, all obviously lies, but no one dated the loss of his virginity as early as Eddie did. He prided himself on this fact and spiced up his story as he grew older and became aware of more and more details of what might actually occur during a sexual experience. Perhaps because of his sensing the need to hide his virginity and because of the great amount of creativity required to do so, sex for Eddie would always be intricately related to his imagination. Sex for him would be story after story that he told to himself, each beginning not with "Once upon a time. . . " but with "I once kissed a girl from California. . . "

But long after most of the other boys' stories began to take on unmistakable rings of credibility, Eddie's continued to be mere fabrications. Even Malcolm had a true story before he did. His lies could be used to save face, but deep down he knew a truth that chilled him to the bone: He was a virgin. It would take an ordinary spring day and a girl named Coco to cure him.

Backyards. He remembers how once he and Malcolm each got a puppy from another boy in the neighborhood whose dog had just given birth to a large litter. The mother was a German shepherd, sort of, but their friend wasn't sure who or what the father was. They took the puppies after just a week because the mother had so many that she seemed to be having trouble feeding all of them. Eddie named his Bingo and Malcolm named his Rocket. Bingo had a solid black coat over most of his body with little white spots on his ears and nose. Rocket was a deep, rich gray with white paws. Both were fluffy and fit perfectly into the arms of nine-year-olds. They kept them inside for a week, feeding them bowls and bowls of milk to give them strength. Then they set up an elaborate system of cardboard boxes beneath the trees in the backyard as a home for the puppies. Using collars made from old leather belts and leashes made from kite string, they tied their pets to a tree to keep them from wandering. It was the middle of March, and the weather was mild. The boys even slept outside with the puppies a couple of times.

"Malcolm," Eddie said on the first night they slept outside with Rocket and Bingo. "You think we gon be able to teach em how to do stuff?"

"Yeah. I think so," Malcolm answered, holding Rocket closely and running his fingers through the dog's gray fluff.

"What you gon teach Rocket how to do?" asked Eddie, Bingo at his side.

"I don't know. All kinda stuff. Maybe how to run after somethin when I throw it and then bring it back to me. Or maybe how to shake your hand."

"Yeah. Like on *Lassie.*"

"Yeah. Like on *Lassie.*"

"But, Malcolm. Lassie a girl dog. Bingo and Rocket is boys."

"So."

"We gotta teach em how to do some boy stuff."

"What you mean, 'boy stuff'? It's all the same thing. Lassie do all kinda stuff."

"I know she do, but. . . " Eddie couldn't finish what he wanted to say. He didn't really know what he wanted to say. And he knew that even if he could say what he felt, Malcolm would say his side and make too much sense to dispute. That was what he always did: He made too much sense for Eddie to dispute.

Malcolm spoke. "I don't see the difference. If we can teach em how to shake somebody hand or how to save people and stuff, that ought to be good. I don't know what else they got to show em how to do. You know somethin else to show em?"

"No," Eddie said. Then, thinking there must be something else, he added, "I don't know."

"Well, if you think of somethin else, tell me. Okay?"

"Okay."

"I'm sleepy. You sleepy?"

"Uh huh, kinda," Eddie replied.

"You scared to sleep out here?"

"Uh uhn," Eddie said, telling the truth. "Ain't nothing to be scared of." He paused. "You scared, huh?"

"A little bit," Malcolm admitted. "It's dark out here."

Eddie sat up and propped his back up against the oak tree. Bingo had fallen asleep at his side, and he was petting the dog lightly. "You go head and go to sleep. I'ma stay up for a while and watch out for us. I ain't that sleepy."

"You sure?"

"Yeah, I'm sure. I'ma watch."

"Okay." Malcolm rolled over and lay on his back and propped Rocket up on his chest. "Goodnight."

"Goodnight."

Not long after that night, the puppies became sick and died. Eddie's father said they must have taken them away from the mother too soon. The boys explained why they had done so, and he told them that it wasn't anybody's fault and that he wasn't trying to blame them. He took the puppies away and buried them someplace; the boys never knew where. Their grief wore off quickly, and now and then Malcolm and Eddie would reminisce fondly about Rocket and Bingo and the month (though it would always seem like so much longer) the four of them shared together.

His hands occupied with carrying the glass of scotch and Princess' greasy ham bone, Eddie wonders how he's going to manage to close the back door behind him. He's already had two glasses of scotch to give himself enough energy to cut the grass. He's not even sure whether or not he'll be able to step down from the house to the concrete pathway and onto the grass without stumbling.

So – *how will he close the back door?*

Chivas Regal gives him a buzz around the third glass. That's why he has only two before he cuts the grass. And if he has to do something more involved than pushing the lawn mower, he has only one. If he has to change the oil in the car, he has only one. If he's messing with the lights or anything having to do with electricity, then it's definitely only one. Anything having to do with money – writing out a check or going Christmas shopping – he does after having only one. Going to work on Monday morning is one plus five or six cigarettes. Tuesday is one plus maybe one or two smokes. By Wednesday, and for the rest of the week, he can usually get by with a couple cups of coffee and a couple cigarettes like the rest of the world. He's about halfway finished with this third glass in his hand now, and he's feeling pretty good. With one drink, he can begin to relax. With two he can become fully relaxed. And somewhere in the middle of the third drink he becomes capable of doing remarkable things, like seeing the hand of God, pinky raised, coloring a sunset orange.

After he closes this back door, he will begin to glide across the grass toward Princess, who will already have seen him with the large bone in his hand and will have started to run around in her yard. She'll stop for a second or two to prop her front paws on the top of the three-foot-high metal fence and look at Eddie, and he'll wave the bone at her. She'll be panting heavily and her long pink tongue will be hanging from her mouth dripping saliva. Then she'll drop from the fence, back away, and pirouette twice before starting her wild scampering about the yard again. She'll run around and around the old two-foot-high stump that is planted in the center of the yard. Eddie loves the way she always goes through such manic motions. He loves Princess. She belongs in this backyard behind his. If he comes out here one day and looks across that fence and she isn't there, then that house of gray bricks where her owners live will not be there either.

How will he close the door?

(Somebody Jenkins is the man's name who lives inside the house, he thinks; he isn't sure. His wife's name is Dorothy. He remembers because she has the same name as his mother. They're in their late forties. Four kids. The oldest is a beautiful, long-legged daughter named Cassandra. They call her San for short. She looks about eighteen and has very smooth black skin. She must be proud of it, the way she wears her hair pulled back off of her face all the time. Eddie saw her up close one day when he came out to feed Princess. He introduced himself and said he had heard that her name was Cassandra. She nodded, but declined to speak to him. She just sat in the lawn chair next to the stump, which had a smooth, eighteen-inch-diameter face, and on top of which rested her misty glass of iced tea. She just sat there and watched him. He told her that her mother had said it was okay if he fed Princess. She nodded again, placed both of her hands on her head, and made a couple of motions that would have smoothed her hair back away from her face, if it hadn't been pulled back so neatly already. He asked her what school she went to, and she told him South End. She looked like a cheerleader to him, he said. She told him that, yes, she was a cheerleader. She liked it okay, she said, after he had asked, but he could tell from the way she was looking away and sighing and pretending to brush flies away from her long, dark, hairless legs that she really didn't want to be bothered with conversation, at least not his conversation. He decided he'd better leave her alone in case she'd caught a glimpse of what was in his mind: her doing a backbend in the nude, legs spread wide, with her behind resting on the stump and him covering her and entering her, whispering in her ear, "Two, four, six, eight. Who do you appreciate?" If she'd seen his lust, she might go inside and tell Daddy what's-his-name. He brushed a real fly from his forehead and turned his attention to Princess, who was busy devouring the chicken bones he had thrown to her.) But Princess is here today, and so are the creamy gray house and the perfectly placed stump.

How will he close the door?

He'll reach the fence and toss the bone to the dog, not a full collie, the woman has told him. Princess has too many brown spots in the white parts of her coat that give her away, the woman says.

The dog will handle the bone in a very playful way. Eddie will smile as he watches her. She will find all of the ham and fat he's made sure is still on the bone. He'll feel the need to light a cigarette and when he reaches to his shirt pocket he'll smell the grease left on his hand from the bone. He'll wipe his hand first briskly across the grass and then casually in the crotch of his dirty old cutting-the-grass jeans. He'll sip the scotch and reach for the cigarettes and lighter. When he flicks the lighter, Princess, startled, will look up at him with quick-fear in her eyes. Seeing only the tiny flame, she'll swallow once with mock haughtiness and glare at Eddie as if to say, "Nigger, please," and when the flame disappears, she'll go back to munching on the bone. Eddie will laugh to himself beneath his smile and draw heavily on the cigarette.

He'll hear other laughter behind him moving closer and closer, and he'll turn to see Tammy in a giggling fit coming toward him in her slow, uncoordinated run. "Daddy," she'll be calling, getting closer. She'll arrive at the fence and stand beside him out of breath. "Daddy–" He'll take one long last drag on his cigarette and then pluck it away. Then he'll squat down and hug her. She'll smell like an Ivory soap bath. "What's wrong?" he'll ask. "What's wrong with Daddy's baby?"

"Da–" She won't be able to catch her breath from the run and the laughter.

"Slow down. What's so funny?"

"Daddy... Edward Junior... he was chasing me," she'll say, starting to calm down.

"Why was he chasing you, that mean old boy?"

"Cuz I was running from him, Daddy. Cuz I didn't want him to be tickling me no more. He keep tickling me, Daddy." She won't be able to stop laughing.

"Well, you tell him I said he better stop tickling you, you hear?"

"Okay, Daddy." Her laughter will slow and turn into heavy breathing.

75

He'll notice she's not wearing any shoes, and he'll playfully slap her on her bare feet. "What happened to your shoes, girl?"

She'll look down at her feet. "I left them in the house. I was running so fast from Edward Junior."

"Well, you watch your step out here. They got a few pieces of wire I saw out here while I was cutting the grass."

"Okay," she'll say.

He'll stand up and lean on the fence to return to watching Princess toying with the bone. Tammy will stay at his side and watch the dog, too. She'll place one hand on the metal fence and the other arm halfway around her father's waist, three fingers hooked on a belt loop at his back. The side of her face will be touching his hip.

"Daddy," she'll say, "when are we going to get a dog?"

Her voice will have changed, the way it does sometimes when she wants something; it still startles Eddie, the way it can go all prissy, white and precocious, like that of a child in a television commercial. His kids will be better than he is; they're learning better; they'll know how to fit in. "I don't know, Tammy," he'll say, not wanting to disappoint her. "Maybe when y'all get a little older."

"Everything is when we get a little older," she'll say sadly.

"Well, we might get one later." He'll nod toward Princess. "Don't you like Princess? She's a good dog."

"Yeah, Daddy. But she's not ours. I want our own," she'll whine a little.

"Well, like I said, we might get one later on." He'll pat her head and press it more closely to her side. They'll watch Princess for a while longer, then Eddie will tell her that it's time for her to go back inside. "Go ahead. It's gonna be dark out here in a little while."

"Aw, Daddy. Let me stay."

"Go on in now. And when I come back in I'm gonna tickle you and your brother both." He'll make a move with wiggling fingers for Tammy's waist and she'll turn laughing and running back toward the house. He'll yell for her to watch her step, and he'll hear her sing, "Ooh, Edward Juniuh-uh. Daddy gon git you-ou."

Then Eddie will face Princess again. He'll shake his glass from side to side and wait to hear the tinkling moneylike sound of ice hitting glass, but it won't come; the ice will have melted along with most of the orange at the horizon, which will by now be mostly smoky blue. He'll decide that he'll down the rest of the glass in one gulp. He'll tip it toward Princess. A toast, he'll think. Like on TV or in the movies. (He'll laugh to himself. He can't really fit in the way Tammy and Edward Junior will be able to, but he can fake it pretty well sometimes.) A toast. A toast to *everything*. Just everything. He wants to see a million more days like this one. Something will move within him. Something from his stomach to his chest. And he'll feel as though his heart is blossoming like some big beautiful rose. He'll want to reach inside, take it out, and show it to someone, but there won't be anyone and he won't know how. So he'll move the glass to his lips instead. To this beautiful day, this beautiful August day – and to you, Princess, to you and your beautiful backyard, and to the beautiful girl who is not there in the lawn chair that is not there next to the stump that *is* there, solid as a rock.

He'll gulp.

With an elbow and the back of a heel, he slaps and hooks the door, and it closes behind him.

AND HE WAS 23 YEARS OLD...

HE AND BETTY and Malcolm and Pam are sitting in a restaurant on the south side of South End having dinner. Betty keeps going on and on about how much she is worried about having to leave the children with her mother for the evening. Tammy is one of those babies who always seems to have a cold, and Betty doesn't know if her mother will be able to handle her if she starts crying to complain about what's ailing her. And Edward Junior was already crying when they left to meet Malcolm and Pam at the movies. Eddie wants to tell Betty to shut up, that she is really being insensitive to Pam's feelings. (Pam had a miscarriage just after she and Malcolm were married about four years ago and since then hasn't had any luck in conceiving, though she has been trying really hard.) Pam is squinting with pain as she listens to Betty and watches a mother go through the sweet agonies of worrying about the well-being of her children. Eddie feels that Pam's pain is perhaps the pain of empathy but more likely the pain of desire and envy. Her teeth are clenched tightly and her light brown eyes have turned stony and opaque. She is toying with a piece of steak with her fork, but she won't eat another bite tonight, Eddie thinks. Malcolm is sort of staring off into the distance, nothing new for him really. And Betty is there, over there. But Eddie's eyes are on Pam in search of some sign of what is going on inside of her. (Together, she and Malcolm are so much better than he and Betty. Not because Pam is at all better than Betty; she isn't; they're about equal. [To him, all women are generally good, so much better than men.] Pam and Malcolm are better because Malcolm, Eddie feels, is so much better than he. In fact, he may even be as good as Pam and Betty.) Earlier, Pam made a quick glance in Malcolm's direction, but it didn't answer any of the questions Eddie has about them. If anything, it only made him more curious. Was Malcolm impotent? Was that what the glance meant? Pam even shifted in her seat after flicking her eyes at Malcolm. Was it shame that was forcing her to find a new position, a position that would not show so clearly her overwhelming inferiority? Was that what was there in her glance and her shifting? That would depend upon whether or not the problem causing her and Malcolm's inability to conceive was one that would cause someone like Pam — a simple woman with a Catholic upbringing that she allows to be prominent but not stifling (in this respect she is akin to Betty) — to feel ashamed. Eddie tests the possibility of his diagnosis of impotency being correct. Is Pam, Eddie asks himself, the kind of woman who, if she has no children and is sitting in a restaurant listening to some fertile bitch go on and on about her precious babies ("And, girl, she keeps a cold, plus she's got some more new teeth coming in. You've got to put that stuff in just right. I've been using — "), and if the reason she has no children is because her husband is impotent, is she the kind of woman who would, on top of gritting her teeth and playing with her steak, glance quickly at her sad hero and, because his impotence is making her feel ashamed, shift her position in her seat? Is she that kind of woman? Yes, Eddie answers. Pam is that kind of woman. Malcolm could be impotent. But Pam, he must admit, might react that way if the problem stems from other circumstances as well. For instance, Malcolm could be sterile. Something could have happened to him since her first pregnancy. Pam's reaction could have been the same if that is the case. And a sterile or an impotent man would be looking away the way Malcolm is now, the way he does so often. But either way, things don't look good for Malcolm. If one of these possibilities is correct, either he can't get it up or he's shooting blanks. But couldn't Pam be the one who's sterile? Does that idea work? Her glance would have been to check her spouse to make sure that he was not betraying her secret; her shifting, some subconscious squirming trying to jiggle the ovaries into action.

But he is being too hard on Betty, right now. God knows she wouldn't hurt anyone. She'd be the last person in the world to intentionally hurt Pam. She obviously doesn't realize what she's doing to her friend. This motherhood thing must be more complex than he can understand. She's so worried about the kids that nothing else matters to her. She's glowing with concern. No malice here, only her private brand of Louisiana charm that comes through in her husky voice as a willingness, a necessity, really, to be frank and shameless about such things as pain and pride. Eddie senses a contradiction here, but retreats: no malice. She's decided to go back to work at the department store; there's an opening finally. Not that she would have gone back much earlier, though – the baby being too young for day care. She starts in a couple of weeks, assistant manager again. Eddie marvels at the way she can keep talking without anybody else doing anything except nodding or going "Mm-hmm," sometimes without even

that. When it comes to social matters – and many other matters – she carries him. She could carry others as well, he believes,
even as heavy a load as he can be sometimes. But she doesn't
even know he exists right now, absorbed the way she is in discussing the babies and how they are affecting her life. Her eyes
are aflame with a passion for those two priceless beings she and
Eddie have created. The brightness he sees in her eyes is most
certainly a fire, but cool with life, a fire that ignites her words and
sends them shooting out like bottle rockets. At times like this one,
when she is speaking and far away from him, he thinks she could
start a revolution, overthrow a government, or make him whatever it is she wants him to be. (He is not so sure what that is exactly, but he knows it has something to do with his becoming a
"better man." And if becoming a better man wouldn't be too painful an experience, then that's a transformation he wouldn't mind
her guiding him through.) Behind her eyes, though, a disturbing
force of some kind is registering. It is dark, hard, cubic, and rest-
less, banging at the back of her skull. And because it is there, in
the place that is so often the origin of headaches, he knows that
this force is himself. Its rumblings occasionally cause one of the
flames in her eyes to flicker, but they both burn on despite the dis-
ruptions. "Betty," he wants to say, "Oh, Betty... I am here. If
you look at me, I won't try to hide myself. I won't be silent. I will
give you something back. I promise. Look. Here – my gift to you is
this: Just look closely at Pam and see her pain. She is hurting because of what you are saying. I know you can usually see things
like this more clearly than I can. But this one time I see it and you
do not. And I know you do not wish to hurt her, so I am showing
you this one thing that I can. Take it, please, and do with it what
you will." This is what he wants to say. This is what is on the tip of
his tongue. Yet he is silent, because, really, what are the words?
What can he say besides "Baby, I love you"? And saying even just
that is such a struggle. But "Baby, I love you" won't say what he
means. It won't say that he doesn't want to be the headache, the

flicker; he wants to be the flame. He wants, he wants, but how to say what he wants? He doesn't know how to say things like "I feel like a horse," even though sometimes that's exactly the way he feels. And if you can't tell her you feel that way, then in her eyes you simply *don't* feel that way. If you don't say it, no one will ever know. But he doesn't know how to say it. What are the words? He reaches deep within himself, all the way back to "Ma-ma," all the way back to "Da-da," but the words he needs aren't there. He needs a dictionary that can read his mind and turn automatically to all the right pages, one that could form the sentences. He would reach for it now, and it would know that he wants to say . . . To say what? Uhm, uhm – he has already lost it. And it was something good, too. Something real good. If he had said it, he would have felt real good. She would have felt real good. And he wouldn't have to feel like a failure, which is how he feels right now. It was that good. But he has lost it. It doesn't really matter, though, because there is no dictionary that can read his mind. And if there is, he doesn't have a copy. So he'll never say whatever it is that he wanted to say. And to avoid the sense that he is a failure, he wipes away even the desire to say it, he wipes away the feeling. Right now this good woman who is his wife will just have to be a bitch. If she is a bitch, being himself is bearable. Tomorrow she can be an angel, maybe even later on tonight. But right now, right this second, she must be a bitch, a bitch whose face he'd like to mold into a cushion that would feel nice against the back of his hand.

And in the corner of Eddie's eye – (where he somehow always seems to be) – there's Malcolm, sterile or otherwise, cool and aloof, staring away and humming along with the Muzak. He is tapping his index finger on his chin, perhaps inventing a bass line. The finger is also pointing to his thin lips, behind which hides a much-coveted cleverness. If he cares to, he can whistle a few words and bring this table some relief. But he won't; he chooses his own moments. Only on rare occasions do his moments coincide with Eddie's. When they do, Eddie feels that he's being taken along for a ride, and for a while he feels that he and Malcolm are inseparable. At such times, Eddie can feel ripples in the air between him and Malcolm, ripples made by an undulating chain of bubbles flowing from Malcolm's slightly opened mouth heading for Eddie's chin, just below his lower lip, where each bubble would burst quietly in a series of baby kisses. But it is never like fags. It is something special, something to hang on to. He wishes it were more like a firm handshake, because then there wouldn't be the confusion. But it isn't like that at all. It's a connection too rare to be compared to something that common – that, plus it is something he isn't entirely sure is as simply masculine as a handshake. In fact, he kind of thinks he and Malcolm might be wandering into a feminine territory of "good" at such moments. And, of course, to Eddie's mind, it is always Malcolm who initiates such a venture.

But none of this is happening right now; their moments aren't coinciding. There is nothing "good" about right now. If he ever has to remind himself of what happened on this night, he'll remember that Betty was talking a lot, that Malcolm was far away, and that Pam kept jiggling in her seat – yes, it was just like Betty had said: these people had their air conditioner turned up too damned high – trying to keep warm.

: 0 4

AND HE WAS 22 YEARS OLD...

HE IS bending down to embrace Edward Junior and to try to quiet the boy down. He must have been having a nightmare or something, if twenty-one-month-old children have nightmares. Maybe he was dreaming about a spanking (a couple of taps on the leg are all Betty ever gives him) or about that television commercial with the fat clown with eyes that pop out and hang from their sockets by springs. Every time that comes on he runs to the back of the house or to Betty. Or maybe he was experiencing some kind of mystical sympathy for the struggle Eddie was having in the room down the hall trying to create a story about how he lost his virginity. Whatever the reason for the scream was, his call for help was an answer to Eddie's own call. It is really a wonder that Betty has never asked that question before. She's hinted around it a few times, but she hadn't asked it directly until tonight, with her soft palm-touch. "Who was it?" she asked. Was he to assume from her mock-jealous tone that whoever had had it first had been, in her eyes, an enviable person? If that was what she meant, then she was most certainly mistaken. Coco was not a person to be envied. And Betty, of course, knew this—but she did not know that her sister was the target of her playful jealousy. Even as she told Coco's story to him moments ago, crying in his arms, she knew what she did not know.

Oh, Eddie, it's so terrible. I don't know if I can tell it . . . the way it happened. That night. I can still remember it like it was yesterday. I mean the whole thing, not just that night. What a big mistake I made! I shoulda, oh, I shoulda—It's my fault. And now . . . my poor sister. I don't know if I can tell it. But I want to tell somebody. It's time to tell somebody. Let me start from the beginning. . . . This was when I was sixteen and Coco was fifteen. It was a Saturday, sometime in May. She had been acting funny all day. But I just figured, Oh, Lord, I'm gonna have to put up with all kinda foolishness until she gets finished with her period. She'd been making a fuss all day about there never being any Kotex in the house when she needed it. She even made a trip around the corner to Tate's and bought a box. When she got back, she went into the bathroom and stayed in long enough to put one on. Came out—and you'd have thought she would have been happy and relaxed a little —but when she came out, looked like she'd been crying. I didn't really pay it no mind, because a period is such a strange thing. It can really hit you hard sometimes. Hell, I know mine has made me cry more than once. (Listen to me. I can't even believe I'm talkin like this. But, shoot, you're a grown man. You know what a period is.) So, anyway, you know, I didn't pay any attention to Coco's foolishness. She was gone most of the day after that with Patricia Jenkins. You remember her, that little ole fast girl that Coco used to hang out with all the time. I see her in the mall sometimes now. I think things turned out all right for her. Married, I think. I think she mighta been a year younger than Coco. They spent the day out shopping somewhere, and they came back with a blouse and a pair of earrings each. That night they went to some party, I think at the Bankses' house. You might remember that night, cuz we talked on the phone and you said you didn't want to go to no party because you were tired and pissed off because Coach Tillis had made y'all practice all day on a Saturday. The state meet was coming up soon. Remember? We talked for almost two hours. And after I got off the phone I went to sleep right away, all happy because I was already in love with you.

I was sleeping, but I heard when she came in. It must have been close to twelve, cuz that was our curfew and Mama was strict about it. Then I guess I went back to sleep, cuz I don't remember her gettin into bed. The next thing I knew she was jerkin on my arm and wakin me up and cryin and carryin on. I asked her, "Girl, what's wrong with you?" She just kept saying, "Betty, Betty, I don't know what to do." I kept asking her what she was talking about, but she didn't make any sense until I finally calmed her down. Then she told me she had missed her period. I said, "How can you say you missed your period when you just started it this morning?" She told me she wasn't on her period, that she didn't know why she had made all that fuss that morning, but that it was all a lie – one big lie. Maybe she was just trying to cover it up. She thought she was probably pregnant. I didn't really know what to say. I knew she wasn't a virgin. And I had warned her that she was getting a reputation by hanging with that Patricia and from doing whatever it was she was doing. But, Lord, I thought she had better sense than to go out and get pregnant. We were quiet for a while, then I said, "Well, I guess you better go wake up Mama and tell her." Then she got all crazy again, started crying, saying how Mama would kill her if she found out – and she was probably right, too. But what choice did she have? Sooner or later Mama was gonna know some-

*thing. Then she told me about how Patricia knew where she could
go to get an abortion without anybody having to know. I told her I
didn't think it was right for her to do something like that without
talking to Mama first, and you just never knew about things like
that. But she said she knew it would work. Patricia had already
done it, she said, which didn't surprise me. When I told her again
that I thought she should tell Mama, she just got hysterical, crying
and making a mess on the pillow. I didn't know what else to do but
tell her I wouldn't tell. She made me promise. "You can't never tell
nobody," she said. And I promised. And I told her I would do what I
could to help her. She fell asleep in my arms like a baby – before I
even had a chance to ask her the obvious question . . . you know,
who the daddy was. And when I finally did get to ask her, she just
told me it wasn't important. But I figured it was Tyrone Banks's.
She had mentioned him a couple of times, and I knew he had three
different babies by three different girls. I wanted to ask her if it was
him but, like I said, she was already asleep. I felt so funny about
having such a big secret from Mama.*

*Well, we went to a doctor, and he turned out to be just a regular
doctor. Nothing horrible. Dr. Powers or Dr. Potter. Something
starting with a P. His office was across town on Sixth Street. We
caught the bus down Broad Street and walked the rest of the way.
She wanted me to stay in the waiting room while the doctor saw
her, so I did. When she walked down the long hall to one of the ex-
amination rooms in the back, she waved to me. And I knew she
wasn't a little girl anymore. She had some pink ribbon in her hair,
but she wasn't a little girl. And when she walked slowly back down
the hall towards me a couple of hours later, I knew she was a
woman. More a woman than I was.*

*Ooh, but, Eddie – I don't know what happened. Two days later
Coco got sick. She said she didn't know what it was, but she just felt
funny inside. She called the doctor and he gave her a prescription
and told her to get back to see him as soon as possible. She didn't
really want to go back, but after a few days she wasn't getting any*

better. So I made her go back. He examined her and told her something had happened wrong. She couldn't remember exactly what he told her. All she knew was that it meant she couldn't have any children. When I tried to get her to remember what the doctor had told her, she would only say, "He just messed up." She didn't really sound like she cared. And the more I think about it, the more I think she really didn't care. That's what changed her. That's what made her get so cold and so bitchy. You know for yourself how she was. I thought it might wear off, but it never did. And then after a while there was just nothin we could do with her. She had so many men and so many boys – just about anything that looked her way. It was so sad and so gross. But she wouldn't listen to me or Mama. She was too grown for that. She knew more than anybody else, or at least that's the way she acted. She knew it all and she didn't give a damn. She didn't have to worry about getting pregnant – so she didn't care. She couldn't look forward to getting pregnant, so she didn't care. She didn't care about nobody because that Tyrone Banks bastard didn't care about her. Some people think it was VD or somethin – but I think it was all that not caring that drove her crazy.

And I have to blame myself for some of it. There's no getting around it. I played my part in it. If I had just told. . . But by the time I realized I should have told, it was too late. And right now, Eddie, if you can believe it – right now is the first time I've ever told. Even though I shouldn't. Because I didn't even tell Mama then, or ever. But I'm glad to be able to tell it now. I'm glad I have you to tell it to. It feels so good.

Betty cannot possibly suspect his reason for uncharacteristically volunteering to check on the baby, that *he* is Tyrone Banks. Isn't this a night when he has "father" written all over his face? And she is, she says, probably pregnant right now. He is only preparing himself for the next baby. This time around he will be more of a help to her. Placing one hand under his son's head and sliding his arm beneath the child's back to cradle him, Eddie allows the boy to grip the index finger of his other hand. The child's crying starts to fade. Lifting the boy to his chest, Eddie feels all of his movements are perfect. But he is not making them happen. He feels that some unknown force has captured the movements like butterflies in a net and is handing them to him as gifts just for being in the right place at the right time. The way he is bending down, the way he is placing his hand here, the way he is sliding his arm there, the way he is putting his other hand there. All perfect, all beyond his control. And even before he does so, he knows he will pucker his lips and blow "shh."

AND HE WAS 30 YEARS OLD...

HE IS passing his cigarette lighter to Edward Junior ("Daddy, what's so funny?"), who is about to light the candles on Betty's birthday cake. The whole little party is the boy's idea and he's visibly excited about having managed to pull it off. (He must have had quite a fright earlier when Eddie didn't come straight from work to pick up the cake from the bakery like he was supposed to. But, when he realized that Eddie must have forgotten about the cake, he just got on his bike and rode the mile and a half down Vincent Road and brought the cake home himself.) His hand is trembling as he reaches for the lighter. A trembling hand. Eddie can't help wincing beneath his laughter. This boy is not turning out right. He'll be ten in a couple of months, right before

Christmas, and here he is trembling with excitement over his mother's birthday. Nothing about the boy reminds Eddie of himself. (Oh, how he was misled by the boy's early mimicking of his own affection for the merry-go-round. That, it turns out, was a fluke.) As skinny as can be, he never seems to gain a pound, just keeps getting taller and taller. His arms remind Eddie of the legs of the television stand in his and Betty's bedroom. Thin and breakable. He is fragile-looking. That's one of the things about him that bothers Eddie. He would break if you hit him too hard or held him too tightly. And he's high-strung; he does everything fast. Fidgety. Too many wasted motions. Eddie is always telling him he needs to slow down. He walks on his toes, too, bouncing up and down. It's annoying sometimes, but Eddie consoles himself with the idea that maybe the strange walk is building up the boy's calf muscles. Up, one. Down, two. Up, three. Down, four. Eddie counts to himself sometimes as he watches Edward walking. Up, one. Down, two. Up, three. Down, four. The exercising might come in handy later. Even though he shows no interest in any real sport yet—he likes tennis—those calf muscles could come in handy when he starts to play basketball or football or run track. There's no telling how many pros started out walking on their toes, developing some important muscles without even trying, without even knowing it. You just have to be lucky, that's all.

The bouncy walk could possibly be a good sign, but Eddie can't reason away the trembling hand. It worries him. It is not the hand of the person he wants his son to be. If he were passing the boy the lighter to fire up a joint, then that hand would be well on its way to being soothed, calmed into the state of equanimity it should always be in. Wouldn't that be a trip, a stone trip? That's what's so funny, my man. You smoking a J. That's what's so funny. S-s-s-sssss. Eddie is laughing his "high" laugh. The laugh that means he has been smoking some good shit or maybe even got his hands on some coke somewhere. S-s-s-sssss. That's how it goes. He just puffs out a few times until the air manages to flow out in a steady stream. He knows he'll have to get control of himself before Betty makes it home. He doesn't feel like hearing her shit. But he is laughing now about his son smoking a joint. He sees the smiling innocent face reaching for the lighter. You will never smoke a joint, he thinks. And I will never be your hero. You will never play ball. You will read books and be better than me and maybe even better than Betty. Yes, you will be one of those men who can be better than women. The way Malcolm was. You're turning out like Malcolm, only better. So Eddie is wrong, he feels suddenly, to say that the boy is not turning out right. What he means to say is that Edward Junior is not turning out the way he turned out. And that isn't so bad. He's turning out to be someone who can make his own dreams come true. Eddie doesn't have to see the pride on Betty's face when she's watching Edward Junior and Tammy without their knowing it to realize that his children's not being like him is a good thing; he knows it. He hates his what-if-I-was-this and what-if-I-was-that dreams. They've become boring and repetitious and they never come true. With these children, the way Betty is raising them, any dream is a real possibility. If Edward Junior dreams something like "What if I was the kind of person who could sit down and read a book by William Shakespeare," he can become that kind of person. If he wants to he can read books by William Shakespeare. All those good books he wrote. And they will be able to remember Shakespeare's name all the time. Something Eddie cannot do. (When he forgets it and needs to remember it to complete a dream, he thinks of men in jungles waving their weapons at one another; they are angry with one another; their weapons are spears; they aren't "waving" the spears; they're shaking them in anger; shaking spears. Shakespeare. What if I could read something by Shakespeare and know what he was talking about?)

And if they dream, "What if I could make a right turn off the interstate onto Cameron Road and drive all the way to the Gulf," their hearts will let them make the turn and go all the way.

What if, Eddie thinks, I could go home right now. Go home to the house on Pine Street. And when I walked through the door, I would suddenly be ten years old like you. And what if I had your innocent face and I was going to surprise my mama with a birthday cake. Daddy is handing me his matches to light the candles and I just can't wait for Mama to come home and be surprised. I can't wait for her to blow out the candles and wish that she was somebody else and that Daddy was somebody else and that the whole world was somebody else because last night he beat her up and I went to the bedroom door and whined like a fool for him to stop it, but he didn't and she had to go to work this morning and be some white people's maid with a black eye and a spot on her lip that wouldn't stop bleeding. So she will walk in talking about how she was on her feet all day and how her bunions is killing her and, Lord, who got cake crumbs all over the floor? ("I ain't about to clean that up. One o' y'all better get y'all ass in here an clean this mess up.") But how surprised she is when she sees the cake and the candles with their dancing flames. And she suddenly realizes that this is her birthday and that this is all for her. She starts laughing and crying and accidentally splits her lip where it was starting to heal. And I can't stop laughing. I'm so happy; I just can't stop laughing. She doesn't have to know that Daddy didn't come home right away like he was supposed to so that we could go and pick up the cake. So I had to get on my bike and ride down the street and pick it up. And, of course, he was driving up just as I got back and I had to rush to get all of the candles on in time. So what's the big joke, marijuana breath? Give me the fuckin lighter. Mama will be home in a few minutes, and she'll be tired because she's under a lot of pressure because they just made her a manager. This will make her happy. She'll be able to ignore you tonight. She won't say a word to you tonight, even when she notices the way you smell – and she will because that mouthwash you use never works. And she'll notice because she loves you so much that even when she hates you she likes to get real close to you. You know what I mean. I know you know what I mean. But she won't say anything tonight. I'm getting you off the hook this time; she'll see all of this, the cake and everything, and you know how she is – it'll give her hope. I know you know what I mean. She'll look at me doing something good, and she won't be able to resist giving you some of the credit for it – because I am, let's admit it, like it or not, part of you. So give me the lighter, you stupid ass, let me make her happy and later you and me can go fire up a J. What say? Trust me. Look at this face. This is not the face of a liar. You and me. After the party. No, shit. Thanks. You dumb muthafucka.

Eddie feels the lighter slide through his fingers. "Thank you, Daddy," he hears.

That's right, he thinks, addressing the voice. Take the lighter. Leave me here laughing. Like a fool, you think. But you'll never feel this good. Go ahead. Walk away from me. Down, one. Up, two. Down, three. Up, four. *S-s-s-sssss.* You'll never feel this good. *S-s-s-sssss.* You'll never be like me.

:05

AND HE WAS 31 YEARS OLD...

HE IS crossing the street in front of his house, St. Anthony Street, and he's about to pop his fingers. He is on his way to the park three blocks away. A grayness that goes with the cool weather is pervasive. He is even wearing his gray sweat suit. There is gumbo on his breath – chicken, shrimp, okra, and sausage. During the middle of the night Betty mumbled something that sounded like "Let me show you how to make a roux... smell... warm... roux...." And she got up around six and went to the twenty-four-hour grocery store and bought all the ingredients she needed; she finished the gumbo before she and the kids left for church. Sometimes, if she hasn't finished cooking before she leaves, he has to watch the pots or check something in the oven. But not today.

Eddie stayed out of the way this morning as she and the kids got ready for eleven o'clock mass. On only a couple of occasions has he gone to Betty's church, and neither time did he find anything there to make him want to go regularly. He was raised in a Baptist church, Mount Zion, the memory of which caused Betty's St. Margaret's to impress him as being bland and insincere. He never says anything about it to Betty, though, because he believes there must be something to it, the way she keeps going back. And, besides, he wants the children to have some kind of religion. If not his (and he can't really say he has one now), then hers will have to do. He kind of likes the way Betty has them whispering in their room at night before they go to bed. He listens to them with purpose sometimes. And, though he's never tried, he thinks that if it is ever absolutely necessary he might be able to stumble his way through the "Hail Mary."

He wonders how Betty will feel to find him gone when they get back from church. She likes him less, he knows. They cuddle at night mainly to keep warm, like last night. And now, in her dreams, "love" comes out "roux." The only thing she'll probably miss is the rice from the rice pot and the second breast and drumstick from the gumbo.

To get to the park he will take the short cut along the right side of the shiny metal fence he is approaching. The fence surrounds a leaf-green house with bright white trim. The big yard to the right of the house consists of a little garden and a wide dirt patch. When the Gordons lived there, that dirt patch was a basketball court. Whenever Eddie passes the house, he automatically thinks about playing ball there. They played on a goal with a thick, wooden backboard and a solid metal rim that had probably been painted orange once but which was now a smooth brown. Your fingers slid over the rim if you could dunk the way Eddie could. And many could. Simon, J. J., Mack, Reese, Charlie, and Malcolm. They used to dunk so much that the rim would come down about twice a week until Reese came by one day with his welding torch and made it solid. After that, all of the dunking they did only brought the rim down to a slight tilt that barely affected your shot. And if you played there all the time it didn't bother you at all. You could tell when somebody wasn't from the neighborhood or didn't play on the goal often. When he took his first few shots, the ball would cling to the rim and do roller coasters. But most guys would make the right adjustments quickly. Sometimes they would attach nets, but most times they wouldn't. The nets never seemed to last long enough to be worth the money. When the guys would first put them up, the ball would get caught in them and just hang there, like a tear refusing to fall. But Simon, shooting all by himself, could break them in in about five minutes. And if they were put up on a Saturday morning, they would be in tatters by Sunday afternoon. The goal was held up almost eleven feet high by a solid wooden pole that looked as if it had been carved from a telephone pole. The pole would splinter your hands if you ran them across it the wrong way. Its bottom lay deep beneath the court, which was the same wide dirt patch he sees now surrounded by the fence. Only then, the dust there never seemed to settle completely. Even in the morning sometimes, when no one had been out there playing yet, Eddie could look across the street from his house and see ghosts swirling around on the court. Now, where the court used to be, there is a wide patch of nothing. Off to the side, even with this autumn chill, there is a healthy garden.

A woman lives there. It seems to Eddie that the whole street is full of women. They move in all by themselves or with their kids, but they almost never have husbands. Or sometimes they do have husbands who don't stay around too long. They die or the women divorce them. He is exaggerating, he knows, because even as he is crossing the street right now he can see Randall Fields outside washing his blue Regal, he can see Joe Taylor raking leaves. But there are women living on both sides of both Joe's and Randall's houses. There is a woman with three children next door to him

and Betty. Almeta is still keeping her spot on the corner warm, refusing to die. And there are others scattered *everywhere*. Are he
and Betty the exception? Of course, not. Both Joe and Randall are
married – happily, it seems. And there are the Kileys, the Henrys,
the Guidrys, Reese and Vicky, the Mitchells, the Kanes, Mark and
Debra right next door. He can't name them all. But he realizes
that if he adds the number of couples up, they would far exceed
the number of single women living on his street. There are quite a
few houses where men live alone. So, why do the women stand
out in his mind? He knows. It is because this woman in the house
where the Gordons used to live put up a fence around the court, a
fence he has to walk around to get to the short cut that will take
him to the park where the new courts are. It is because Almeta is a
spooky old bitch. It is because lately Betty has a look about her
that says she might soon want a garden of her own, and neither of
his thumbs is green.

What if he turned around right here in the middle of the street
and went back home to be there when Betty and the children got
back? Wouldn't that be something? He could turn his hip strut
into a quick little jog, pirouette and snap his fingers as though he
were just realizing he had forgotten something important inside
the house. No one will notice his change of heart if he does it that
way; Randall won't miss a dirt spot on his car, and Joe won't miss a
dead leaf. He is seriously considering the notion. The muscles in
his legs tighten in anticipation of a change of motion; the fingers
of his right hand are ready to come together and go "pop." But he
is also considering what is waiting for him at the park. He will be
one of the first to arrive because it's still pretty early. But there will
be some younger people out shooting on the concrete court, just
waiting for enough guys to gather up to start a real game. And it
wouldn't be long before others, having returned from church or
having arisen from their Saturday-night, Sunday-morning stu-
pors, would pack the court. Bodies would fly and sweat would
flow. He would be bruised or maybe even injured. He might crash

to the ground after a rebound and burn his knee on the merci-
lessly solid court. He might come down after a dunk and land
clumsily, spraining an ankle. He might butt heads with an overly
zealous defender ("Foul, muthafucka! Mah ball. . . . "), or he
could jam his finger trying to catch a teammate's pass. But in
some way pain would come. A hard pain that would diminish
quickly with a victory or magnify with a defeat and that either way
would make him breathe more deeply, feel more alive. Cars would
slowly accumulate around the park. The doors would open and
out would come the music and the beer-y, wine-ish laughter of
Sunday afternoon. Many faces and bodies at least ten years younger than his, but some even older, would emerge from the cars.
They would flirt – flash their lashes, stick out their tongues and
touch, hand to hip, thigh to thigh. Before tomorrow, before Monday, they will have every drop of what is theirs. If Chester is there
in his black Seville, Eddie will crawl into the back seat and get
high with whoever else and on whatever is in the car. And before
coming back home he'll play another game to air himself out.

He knows what is waiting for him at the park. But what if he
doesn't go? What if he doesn't cross the street at all? He could do
the jog, the pirouette, the finger pop. He could be home when
they get back from church. He could wash the dirty bowl he left in
the sink. He could be home. What if. . . he could. But the decision has already been made – a long time ago it seems. There will
be no quick jog, no pirouette. The muscles that were preparing for
the turn relax during the same stride that they began to tighten;
they must have known all along. But for some reason the fingers
of his right hand are determined to have their way. He can't stop
the "pop," so he lets it fly and picks it up with a tune that goes
through his brain like a flash of lightning –

"Pop"   "Pop"   "Pop"   "Pop"
      I've got   sun – shi – i – ine . . .
"Pop"   "Pop"   "Pop"   "Pop"
On a clou – ou –   dy   da – ay. . . .

AND HE WAS 21 YEARS OLD...

HE IS turning the dial on the portable radio he brought with
him into Charlie's truck to help make the gathering seem more
like a celebration: Charlie is getting married tomorrow morning.
Charlie is seated in the driver's seat and Malcolm is in the middle.
Malcolm is laughing at something, but Eddie doesn't know what
it is. He heard what they said, but he wasn't really paying attention. Besides, his head is starting to buzz from the wine. They're
passing around the third bottle right now. Some red, bitter-tasting
shit that has Eddie's tongue shriveled up the way eating unripe
persimmons from a tree in the playground of his elementary
school used to. The stuff is nasty, but it's definitely getting the job
done. Malcolm probably doesn't even know what he's laughing at,

with his no-drinking ass. He's probably the highest one in the truck.

Eddie hates it when the black radio station goes off the air at eight o'clock. When it goes off, he usually just shuts off the radio. But sometimes he can catch another good station out of Lafayette. He's trying to keep the party going, so that's what he's doing right now – even though they are well beyond the point where they need music to make the party. When is South End going to get a twenty-four-hour black station? he wonders.

His ashy hand on the dial reminds him that it is cold out. The liquor has made him forget; being packed so tightly next to Malcolm in the truck has warmed him and has made him forget. The street lamp in front of Charlie's apartment is making it easy to see in the truck. His ashy hands, a tear in the cuff of his leather jacket, and out of the corner of his eye, impressions in the dust on the dashboard – his fingerprints. Charlie has had this truck for about two years now. He got it right around the time he and Brenda started seeing a lot of each other. He must have felt like he needed something to drive her around in. And now he's taking the big step. Is that how it works? But a truck, get married? No. That's dumb. Malcolm got married mainly because Pam was pregnant. They were in love, but marriage wasn't in their plans; they were first-year college students. He and Betty got married mainly because they were in love. Really in love. Two years on January the seventh. And they have a beautiful baby boy to prove how much in love they are. It's still a strange feeling to think of himself as a "husband" and as a "daddy." (When he says these two words to himself, they get thrown around in his head in echoes; it is Betty's voice saying "husband," but it is only his own saying "daddy.") But he believes he'll get used to the feeling. The responsibility scares him sometimes. But when it does, he just holds on tightly to Betty, closes his eyes, and forces the experience of living to turn into one long slow-drag, the two of them chest to chest and cheek to cheek. Together, the crowd doesn't seem so large. Together, the two of them don't seem so lost. On Sundays, before it turned cold, they would walk hand in hand on the beach. He would carry the radio in his right hand. She would carry the baby hugged on her left side. One Sunday in June, they were a family strolling on the beach. The sun was blazing, making the sand feel like hot coals beneath their feet, but also brilliantly splashing light on the ripples in the lake. And the hypnotic, undulating motion of the waves called to them to come and wade in the coolness. He and Betty hesitated – as always – neither knowing how to swim. Always drowning on the mind. Always drowning. But Eddie tossed his head toward the water and took a step in that direction; Betty made a move to follow but put her foot down the wrong way, turning her ankle. She looked as though she would fall with the baby in her arms, so without thinking about it, Eddie tossed the radio away and locked his arms around Betty's waist, preventing her and the baby from falling. "Are you all right?" he asked. "Yeah," she said. "This boy's just getting too big to carry, that's all." She was breathing heavily. She never could take too much physical exertion. He both loved and hated this trait in her. He loved it because its existence meant that she, in all situations requiring physical strength, would turn to him for assistance; he hated it because the void made by the lack of physical development was almost certainly filled by an unfathomable emotional depth. Nature worked that way, he knew. "Then put him down and let him walk the rest of the way." She had already let Edward Junior slide down her side to the ground. He plopped himself down on the sand and began playing with it by the fistfuls. "You baby him too much," Eddie said. He was looking around for the radio. He found it ten feet in front of him, a muffled static playing into the sand. When he picked it up he noticed that it had landed on an empty quart bottle of Budweiser. The clear plastic panel that covered the numbers for the frequency levels had a long crack across the FM portion from 98 to 102. And there was a one-half-inch deep jagged indentation in the round metal dial used to change channels. He began turning the dial, trying to find the black station. It was easy, and his thumbnail fit right into the jagged mark on the dial, the way it fits there now. And here he is turning to 95 FM – "The station that's good for your soul" – when he knows that it is off the air for the day. Just a few minutes ago he heard that great theme song with something about the end of the day and some brother blowing the hell out of a saxophone, and then the announcer came on before the song was over (they did that sometimes) and messed it up with that business about kilowatts or some such shit. It had pissed him off without his even knowing it; he was busy swallowing the bitter wine at the time it happened. ("Say, y'all remember Jake," Malcolm was saying. "Jake-and-cake!" Malcolm and Charlie erupted in laughter. "Ah, man... Jake-and-cake...." Laughter.) The station is off the air, but he is turning right back to it. He just turned away, but now he's turning right back. He just did this, he feels. I just did this, he thinks. He is noticing for the first time how his thumbnail fits the mark on the dial; he is noticing for the hundredth time that Malcolm and Charlie are laughing. Oh, yeah. Now he knows. Jake-and-cake. That's it. That's why they're laughing. Jake-and-cake.

Eddie feels a smile coming over his face. There is happiness here. Charlie is getting married. That is good. And they're getting so fucked up. That is good, too.

: 0 6

AND HE WAS 20 YEARS OLD...

HE IS opening the bathroom door to exit the saunalike atmosphere his long, hot shower has created. Wrapped around his neck is one of the new beige towels with the gold embroidered initials on them that someone gave him and Betty for a wedding present. His whole world is new. He is a newlywed, married only two days ago. He left the ranks of the teenagers only a few days before his wedding. This little one-bedroom apartment is new and freshly painted. And the new year itself is still young enough to be considered *new*. How innocent he is, how playful, how clean. In the shower, under the streaming warm water, he scrubbed every inch of his body, wanting to be clean and perfect, smelling brand new to be worthy of existing in his new world. He had a challenge to meet, a wife to support; he was a man now. He took long, slow, deep breaths as he showered, allowing his chest to fill with excitement and the hope of success in an attempt to drown all of his anxiety. He told himself he would have a different attitude toward his job because now he would have something to work for. He and Betty would both be working together to build something strong – stronger. They were already the best of friends. He always knew where she stood with things; she always told him what she thought. Any misunderstandings were quickly cleared up. That's why he married her. She didn't bullshit like other girls he knew; she didn't play games. She never hung up the phone in his face and then called back two minutes later crying about how sorry she was. She was what you'd call mature. He never got anywhere with her by displaying the coolness he had learned to use on girls. Whenever he would slip into this slyness, with just the right voice, she would read his intentions and automatically turn him off. She would roll her eyes away and start looking up at the light on the ceiling or out through a window. Her behavior disturbed him at first because he thought he had the key to succeeding with all women. But in time he learned that what she wanted was for him to be himself, to be for real. Being himself was, however, no easy feat for Eddie; indeed, he had trained himself not to be himself. Being himself would mean having to be consistently original. It would mean having something new to say to her every time he was with her. This was something he would have to learn. He began by letting her take the lead in their relationship, letting her show him the kinds of things he should say, the kinds of things he *could* say. (This was the real key. This was what he should have learned a long time ago, instead of simply becoming infatuated with his own voice.) And so he let himself learn enough to get by. He learned her rules. Or maybe the rules didn't belong to her exclusively, maybe they were universal. The rule he liked best was that many times he shouldn't say anything at all. (This, too, he should have learned before.) He adhered firmly to this principle at times when he was uncertain of the situation. And with Betty, he felt uncertain a great deal of the time. He didn't know what to say to get her to kiss him. His perfect voice worked only about one-fourth of the time. Silence worked about half of the time, so he used it more often. It was a struggle for him not to whisper in her ear about how much he loved her (long before he really did love her), but he knew she wouldn't buy it. And when he finally did say "I love you," while actually *meaning* it, the result was only a long hug. He had felt hurt, cheated, and more than a little pissed off – and more in love than ever before. He came back to her the next day and didn't say a word, and they made love together for the first time. He couldn't predict her reactions, but he sensed within her a self-contained consistency, something that was and always would be beyond his complete comprehension. The day he proposed to her he went to church with her and went through all of the motions of kneeling, standing, sitting, making the sign of the cross as best he could – all in an effort to win some of the influence of her god. He had no idea how she would respond to his proposal. When she said "Yes," he said "Amen."

He hoped that after marrying her and living with her for a while he would be able to understand her better, but he knew there was no guarantee he would. She already understood him, he felt – sometimes better than he understood himself. He knew he would have to struggle to meet the demands of the marriage; Betty's demand that he be original was a difficult one to meet, because (he told himself) he was such an unoriginal person. But she was worth it, worth whatever pain there would be. And there she was last night surprising him yet again with the way she came to his rescue. He had been struggling during his sleep; he couldn't find a comfortable position. And then, as he lay on his stomach, he felt the electricity run through the middle of his body, the tiny stream of lightning flow through him, and his penis became a rock-solid knot. It became uncomfortable for him to remain lying on his stomach, so he had rolled over and felt Betty's soft, smooth skin splash against his own. He had kept rolling until he covered her. She had given a slight push, then slowly put her arms around him and took him inside her. Just thinking about it as he stood under the shower gave him a hard-on. He used his hand to protect himself from the pellets of spraying water, but he let the overflow stream down around the curves of his balls, finding some physical stimulation to match the sensations in his mind. (The shower trick went all the way back to Joey Baptiste, who had taught the entire eighth grade the value of long, warm, soapy showers. After physical education class, they would all be late for their next classes. The coaches used to have to run the boys out of the shower. It got so bad that Coach Jamison actually started timing them as they showered, allowing them only five minutes each.)

And now as he is opening this door, every drop of mist touches off nerves and his body remembers. It remembers the shower, where he remembered last night. If Betty is in the hallway or the bedroom he'll make no effort to cover his bulge, just to see her reaction. Maybe last night was a fluke. But then again, maybe it wasn't. Maybe she just wanted it to be official before she would be his whenever he wanted her, no questions asked. The mere suggestion of this thought is enough to convince him that she *is* his now, that she may even belong to him. He thinks of his mother, his father. Betty is a woman, he is a man. Last night was merely their way of finally admitting this to each other. He tells himself she expects him to take the lead now. He will walk out of the bathroom and tell her how much he really loves her, because he really does and because he should, because a man should say "I love you" to a woman. He'll say it in a sexy voice, his sexiest voice, the way a man must say it. And, because they have this understanding now, after last night, she'll know what to do when he says it; she will not cheat him, she *cannot* hurt him. He is a man, she is a woman.

As he opens the door he is rushed by cooler, drier air and he breathes deeply. Betty is in the kitchen, he senses. He will put on his robe and then go to her with his tender, husky "I love you." All he has to do is follow the breakfast smells – the bacon, the eggs, the coffee and – mmm – the down-home smell of grits. He will go to her now.

AND HE WAS 32 YEARS OLD...

HE IS making one quick flip through Betty's women's magazine before he goes through it slowly and decides what he'll read in it first. He is flipping with his left hand, so the pages are falling from the back cover to the front cover. It is a carefree, fraction-of-a-second flip that is a stream of colors, faces, words, phrases, and even sentences.

The advertisements provide the most beautiful and eye-catching images in the magazine. On the back cover there is a golden box containing a new hair permanent for women. It promises softer and silkier hair. "Create a new and better you." They're offering a two-dollar rebate for each box a consumer buys. The back cover falls and inside Eddie sees a bright blue sky with light wisps of clouds scattered perfectly. The sky is met at its horizon by a blue-green sea that is splashing in the foreground upon a sandy beach, where a man in red swimming trunks is chasing a woman in a pineapple-yellow bikini. They are inviting readers to visit the Bahamas. Trips are available for as low as $299. This is on page 107. On the next page Eddie sees the photograph of a woman he recognizes from a television show. There is a caption below the picture, but the woman's eyes captivate his attention for this fraction of a fraction of a second, and the only phrase of the copy he is able to glimpse is "will appear on."

Pages continue to fall – sometimes one-by-one and sometimes in clusters:

P A G E 105, a jumble of words; the end of an article probably

P A G E 104, more words; a little above the middle of the page: "if it will result in the destruction of the"

P A G E 90, a pink box of Kotex and an ad (His older cousin Valerie was in the back bathroom, the one without a lock, and he opened the door to see her with her underwear down around her left ankle and her right foot propped on the toilet seat as she held her hands to her crotch, sort of examining herself, he thought. She looked up quickly with a startled look on her face and something like terror in her eyes. Her mouth was open, wanting to scream, it seemed, but nothing was coming out, not even a soft breath. He, too, stood frozen and breathless at the sight of her. He knew she wasn't doing anything nasty; she was doing something necessary. Something in the air told him so. Something sweet, pure, and innocent. They were surrounded by a clean silence. He wanted to kneel down before her on the cracked tile floor and remain there until she told him it was okay to rise. He wanted to give her some form of praise because she was doing something not only for herself, he felt, but for him. The

119

pink box on the sink with the word on it that started with a K
was part of it. A part of her and this silence and this sweetness. He was six years old.)

PAGE 89, a picture of a black man; it is surrounded by words

PAGE 88,   more words; near the bottom left side of the page: "and
if there ever was a man with more reason for"; "even
worked for a while as"

PAGE 87, "diamond rings on each hand to match the cuff links
that flash when the light"

PAGE 86, a full-page picture of the black man with a big smile on
his face, one of his front teeth has a gold cap on it; a headline
above the picture – "Lottery"

PAGE 70, a beautiful bronze woman in a black, slippery-looking
evening gown gripping a bottle of liquor by the neck; if there
is a headline for the ad, Eddie doesn't notice it

PAGE 71, the page opposite the woman with the bottle; there is
not a beautiful bronze woman in a slippery-looking evening
gown gripping a bottle of liquor by the neck (She was standing on a corner. She was always standing on a corner – holding the bottle. It was dark, but there was enough light to
stretch her shadow, long and narrow, toward him. What
street is this? he always wondered. I've walked it a million
times, but what street is this? She was looking away, not
high enough to be looking at the stars; her eyes were at just
the right level to see the tops of the magnolia bushes in the
yard where the pink house was. Did she want to pick a
flower? Something for her hair? He knew he wouldn't have
to take a step in her direction; she'd notice him the moment
he landed on this street with his black tuxedo, black leather
shoes, white gloves, and top hat. He didn't know where he
had been before he was on this street; he was just suddenly
here. He never knew who the woman was on the corner.
She was just there to look away at the magnolia bushes for
what seemed hours and hours, and then at the end, turn to

him and say, "Kiss me, you fool." But she couldn't possibly have been looking away for hours and hours – at least not while he watched – because the second he arrived she knew he was there. And at that very second she would turn to him and say, "Kiss me, you fool." But he would never get to kiss her. He never took one step on this street. He would awake right after the woman had spoken to him to find beside him Betty, now, to his dream-heightened sensations, a tepid, muddy puddle of a woman.)

PAGE 63, words, "if your mate has a score"

PAGE 62,   more words, some numbers: 1, 2, 3, 4, 5, 6, 7, 8, 9, 10; part of the headline: "How Androgynous Are You and"

PAGE 58,   a shiny blue car, two-door, with spoke mags; "Taste"

PAGE 57,   "I never want anything like that"

A slip of paper flies out of the magazine.

PAGE 56,   "inside my heart"

PAGE 50,   "to be a star after"

PAGE 48,   "dessert" (He was turning to look out the window at the empty set of monkey bars in the middle of the school playground. It was hot in the classroom. Though the ceiling fans were whirling, there was only a slight honeysuckle breeze. Summer was approaching, and school would be out soon. He could hear Mrs. Brown in front of the class saying "Who can spell – " It was going to be a question. A spelling question. Sometimes she would stop in the middle of a story she was reading to the class and ask a question like that. If she was reading a story about a man who was walking down the street, she might stop and ask if someone could remember how the man was dressed. If the story had someone who owned a dog in it, she might stop after a while and ask, "Now, what was the name of Laura's dog again?" Eddie never answered any of her questions, even though he sometimes knew the answers. He knew there were others who would be able to answer the questions. Malcolm always knew the answers, the show-off muthafucka. Carmen Sampson and Marshall Ames knew the answers, too. But neither Carmen nor Marshall will answer this question. This one belonged to Malcolm. Malcolm knew Mrs. Brown's pattern of quizzing her students so well that the "I" of his "I can" would be out before she could finish asking the question. Malcolm *had to* answer this one. He *had to*. And when he did there would be for Eddie a confirmation about the utter wonder of the universe. He would know that when he had sat daydreaming at the start of the school year and experienced this moment – promising himself he would remember it and that when it actually happened he would smile to himself about his good fortune in capturing one of these things without its being able to do anything to stop him from knowing of its secret existence – he would know that he was right about it all. Malcolm had to answer this question, and as he did so, Eddie knew he would be turning to look out the window [where a leaf would come to rest on the ledge], turning to look out at the empty monkey bars [where a single bird would land]. As he was turning toward the window he heard: "Who can spell –" "I –" "*dessert?*" "can." A leaf fell. A bird landed. His heart leapt. Yes! Oh, yes! There is something weird, something wonderful about this world, and I know it, I know it, I know it!)

PAGE 47, a picture of a steaming hot pie with a red filling that looks like cherries; one slice has been cut and placed on a saucer; there is a fork beside the saucer

PAGE 46, "and she placed her hand under the bed"

PAGE 45, "unafraid"

PAGE 44, "yellow stains"

PAGE 43, a picture of a young black man handing a Coke to a young black woman

PAGE 42, "had been embarrassed at the time"

PAGE 41, "was a passion, a passion which could"

06

PAGE 40, a picture of a black woman holding a box with another woman on its cover; "The Perfect Hair"

PAGE 39, "a woman in her late thirties"

PAGE 38, a pencil sketch of a woman standing in the middle of a large living room, looking up to the ceiling; she looks as though she could be dancing; a headline is above the picture: "*Amy*, by Martha Hall"

The slip of paper that has flown out of the magazine startles Eddie, but only briefly; he knows it is only a subscription solicitation form.

PAGE 32, two small children at a computer; "Buy a future"

PAGE 31, thick black print alternating with regular type; he knows this is the question and answer section that he loves so much because it is filled with advice about sex; this is probably what he'll read first

PAGE 30, in dark print: "My husband has this"; headline: "Your Questions/Our Answers"

PAGE 25, a picture of a woman caressing a container of roll-on deodorant

PAGE 22, a picture of three balloons rising up in the air – one red, one white, one blue; the caption begins: "The best things come"

PAGE 18, a poem, the title is "This Kiss"

PAGE 16, a picture of a woman with a man standing behind her, running his fingers through her hair; "Get the touch," the caption reads

PAGE 13, "every day, but as for"

PAGE 12, "radio station that had the courage"

PAGE 11, "since you could always find"

PAGE 10, a picture of a woman with headphones on, talking into a microphone

PAGE 8, letters; "Katie Briscoe, San Antonio, Texas"

PAGE 7, more letters; "a vacant lot was sold"

PAGE 4, more letters; headline: "Letters to the Editor"

PAGE 3, a table of contents; "*Amy,* a short story by Martha Hall, page 38"

PAGE 2, the inside cover, a beautiful woman and a bottle of shampoo.

PAGE 1, the cover, another beautiful woman; many pretty words
The subscription slip lands in Eddie's lap.

: 0 7

AND HE WAS 33 YEARS OLD...

HE IS standing on the shoulder of Cameron Highway beside his car, a Chevrolet, which has its front end in a ditch. He is
only a few miles from the Gulf and the wind is brisk. His jacket is
ballooning at his back. The darkness is being carved into dancing
shadows by musical red and yellow lights. He hears voices speaking into radios. He hears static. His fear is that they are watching
him too closely, that they will see or perhaps have already seen his
eyes, that they will smell his breath.

What is he doing all the way down Cameron Highway? How did
he get here? He must have driven miles and miles from the I-210
exit ramp. He must have taken the right turn. He must have followed the tug at his chest that told him not to take the left turn

and go home, but to take the right and go to the Gulf. He knows how that feeling comes over him all the time at a certain moment when he is coming off the interstate on his way home. He always feels the gravity-like force pulling him in the direction of the Gulf. His dreamy vision comes to him – as though a fairy has sprinkled a magic dust in his eyes – his vision of ships waiting for him at the shore and men who look like relatives waving for him to hurry. A silly, childish vision, he tells himself. Something out of a picture book. But today he couldn't separate it from reality. Maybe it was the scotch on the rocks he had at B&B's, the little bar on Texas Avenue next to Weldon's grocery store. Maybe that's what did it to him, made him drive out here to get trapped in the middle of nowhere. The gin and seven. The draft beer. The scotch. Maybe.

He stopped at Bob's on his way home from work; it is so tough to go straight home these days. He doesn't feel there's any purpose to his being there very much. He doesn't feel there is any need to be there at all. He's usually the first one home, and when he opens the front door and walks into the empty house he hates that he cannot close the door behind him and lock it forever. He knows they will trickle in slowly – Tammy and Edward Junior, then Betty. And when they are finally gathered, he will feel like an outsider – just a guest. The way they go out of their way to make him feel at home. It's all so awkward. It's as if they don't really know him. He's a stranger to his whole family, he feels. And Betty seems to hate him. He knows she doesn't really, but she is totally removed from him now. She can make a place for him to eat and lounge and sleep, but there is no place for him in her heart. This isn't hatred, he understands – just love gone cold. When they make love, she seems to let her mind wander to thoughts like "What time is it?" and "I wonder when he's gonna be finished." Beneath him, to the touch of his hands and every other part of his body, she feels like a whore. This is what they've come to. He wants to grab her and shake her and ask her what the fuck she wants him to do. Why doesn't she at least talk to him anymore?

7

Yell, scream, do something to make him know what he is doing wrong, the way she used to do. Shit! Can't she help him? He needs help. He wants to strangle her. He wants to punch Edward Junior and cave in his muscleless chest. He wants to slap Tammy into next week. If he could do these things, if he could be cruel enough, then they would have a reason he could understand for treating him like an outsider. Maybe then he would understand why he has no place among them. But he cannot see anything that he has done to provoke their shutting him out. He is a good person. He is a good father. He is a good husband. He is just a little bit confused, that's all. He just needs a little help. But he could never strike any member of his family, even though there's this crazy part of him that wants to. He could never do that. He has rarely had to strike anyone throughout his entire life; he's not a fighter. (He can admit this to himself now, at last: He's not a fighter. He is man, but he is not a fighter. You can *not* be a fighter and still be a man. He knows this now for the first time, and, oh God, what a relief and a pleasure it is to know it.)

So he goes to bars on his way home from work looking for the strength to go home. And he usually finds it. But today something strange happened at B&B's. When he entered through the darkly tinted glass doors, he walked straight to the bar and found a seat on one of the stools there. He ordered a scotch on the rocks. There was a lively Friday happy-hour crowd in the place. The small stereo system could just barely be heard over the chatter. Eddie lit a cigarette and took a long drag. And with that one long inhalation, he could feel the outside world begin to loosen its grip on him. He didn't feel so dirty with the odors and grit of the oil refinery. He didn't feel that when he left he would have to be going anywhere in particular. And when he exhaled the smoke through his nose, he felt suddenly free, like a runaway train. The bartender brought his drink and Eddie quickly swallowed half of it. He put the glass down on the bar top and stared at his hands as they tapped along with the mumbling melody of whatever song was playing. His hands were moving with a hypnotic rhythm. He couldn't hear their tapping, but he imagined the soft dull tones of tough flesh meeting smooth, polished wood. His hands seemed to be strangely separate from him. They appeared to be not his own. They were dancing in a faraway place to a tune so faint he was being forced to imagine most of it. Their being so removed wasn't at all frightening for him, but enchanting; they were having such a good time. He kept watching them as they played in their own world. What weird experiences he had sometimes. Was this normal? How crazy he was to play this game. People might be watching him. He might have looked suspicious sitting there staring at his hands. Maybe he had said something out loud without realizing it. That was stupid. Of course, he hadn't done that. (And even if he had, no one would have been able to hear him.) Only crazy people did that. And he wasn't crazy. He was only sober, and he was in here to take care of that. They were all here to take care of that. But he was smiling. A sober grown man sitting in a bar smiling at his hands. Now that might be a little suspicious looking. Maybe someone had his eyes on Eddie after all. He swiveled slightly to his right and looked up to see if he was being watched – and that was when the strange thing happened. It happened in a flash, but it most certainly happened. When he looked up he saw a line of profiles and backs and backs of heads. His eyes quickly scanned down the row of unknowns until they reached the end of the bar and set firmly – if briefly – on a frighteningly familiar face. A chill flew through Eddie, who refused to believe his own eyes, for, staring back at him, smiling his inimitable smile, was Malcolm – dead for almost six years. Yes, he was dead. Eddie had seen the body with his own eyes. He had seen the blood. And yet here he was now, Malcolm, smiling at him across this smoke-filled room. A scream was caught in Eddie's throat. Water instantly flooded his eyes, blurring his vision. He blinked to clear his eyes, and when he opened them he no longer saw Malcolm at the back of the room. All that he could see, as far as he could see, was a wall made of mirrors. And in the mirrors, he saw faces, fronts, a line of opposite profiles, and finally, not Malcolm, but a reflection of himself – rigid, but for some reason smiling. He couldn't understand the strange mixture of his feelings. The joy and the fear. The hopefulness and the sense of doom. His eyes had played a crazy trick on him, and he liked it and hated it at the same time. He wanted to pick up his glass of scotch and hurl it violently at the mirror and see it all fall into a million pieces of shiny nothing. But he also wanted to take a long slow walk toward the mirror and watch his image gradually get bigger and bigger until he was face to face with himself. He wanted to touch his nose to the other nose and then keep walking through to whatever lay on the other side. The mirror would not shatter; it would take him in and close quietly behind him, and he'd never be missed. No one would even know that he had ever existed. He was nobody's husband, nobody's father, nobody's son, nobody's friend. Nobody.

When he turned to finish his glass of scotch, he was still smiling. He didn't know what he was about to do, but whatever it was, it would be something for him to cheer about. He began to drink quickly. He ordered a gin and seven. By the time he had finished that, he was starting to feel good. Then he had a draft beer because somebody had just offered to buy one for everyone. Finally, he ordered another scotch, because that's the way he always drank; he liked to finish the same way he started. Leaving the bar, he felt light and pure – a breeze whose only chore was to carry the scent of rain.

He never felt guilty about driving while he was drunk. The only person he had ever caused any harm was himself, and even that was only a few scratches. He had totaled his El Camino a while back when he was drunk by crashing into a telephone pole on Simon Boulevard. He had gotten a friend to tow the wrecked car for him and no one ever knew. He even managed to keep it from Betty. He told her the cut on his forehead was from something that happened at work. And she thought the car had simply finally broken down for good, and she was glad to see Eddie get rid of it. He still missed the old car from time to time (he really believed it would probably still be running were it not for the wreck), but he was getting accustomed to the Chevy.

Once he had managed to flop himself into the car, he started it without hesitation. The car had a good FM radio and, since it was always on, it blasted with the ignition. He was feeling so high now that the volume didn't bother him at all. He began to drive out of the parking lot. He was trying to sing along with the radio, but he didn't really know the words. He had heard the song only a couple of times, and its chord progressions weren't quite a part of him yet. He would have to hear it two or three more times before he would be able to put the words and the music together and sing along. As he drove past the giant red neon Weldon's sign, he began to create silly, meaningless lyrics, fitting them into the music of the song as best as he could. "There's a big fuckin sign and the fuckin L ain't even workin. I-I-I wonder. Sometimes I wonder . . . When will they fix it? Will they ever fix it? Turn on the L. Somebody please. Somebody p-p-p-please turn on the L." He drove onto Macon Road and then onto the interstate only a couple of miles from his house, a straight shot away. His exit was the Cameron Highway exit. He stopped noticing the exit sign at the side of the interstate years and years ago. He simply drove until he saw the Exxon station and the McDonald's off to the left. The exit was to the right. It was down this ramp that the desire to drive to the Gulf would overwhelm him. It was a longing that was always there, that always seemed to have been a part of his traveling down this ramp. If there was ever a time when at least a twinge of yearning had not existed, he did not remember it. And yet he had never been to the Gulf of Mexico. He couldn't begin to describe it. The vision conjured by the desire (a desire that could sometimes be shooed away as easily as a fly, but that at other times had to be negotiated with like a creditor), this vision told marvelous stories of ships and beautiful waters. It told of the waving arms and shouting and cheering. It told of travel. It was a vision of desire.

The exit ramp was two-laned. The left lane allowed you to turn only left. The right lane gave you the option of either left or right. He drove down the ramp in the right lane toward the stoplight. Left or right? His mind must have been fading in and out of waking (he was loaded) because by the time he realized what had happened, he was already past the Carrolton Elementary School, where Tammy went to school. He had turned right. Had doing so required strength or weakness? He wasn't sure. All he knew was that a crucial moment was behind him. Onward to the Gulf and then to faraway places that most people could only dream about.

Then he must have faded out for a while. He was awakened with a jolt. His body was flip-flopping across to the passenger side of the front seat. He landed on the floor on his back with his head against the glove compartment.

Standing in the whirling lights, he wants to take off running for the water. He can smell it. He is almost there. But he hears a policeman saying into his radio, "Drunk as a skunk." He is not almost there. He is not moving at all. He is only here.

Here – here.

AND HE WAS 19 YEARS OLD...

HE IS sitting on the edge of his bed tying the laces of his right tennis shoe. It is a few minutes after eleven, and he is on his way out. His mother and father are watching television in the den, which is not completely separated from Eddie's bedroom. There is only a wall that stops about two feet before it reaches the ceiling. And there is no door separating the two rooms, only a wide walkway, which leads to a door to the outside. This part of the house is considered the back. The other two bedrooms (his parents' and Jackie's) are on the far side of the kitchen and the living room.

They must be watching the late movie, he thinks. Some nights they just sit there, his father in the lounger and his mother on the sofa, and watch for hours. They both usually fall asleep there. Anything, Eddie believes, to keep from having to go to bed together. How they hate each other. How they love each other. Once he was peeking over the top of the wall separating his room from the living room, standing on his bed – he must have been nine years old – and he had a view of his mother standing at the kitchen counter chopping onions. His father was sitting in a favorite chair falling asleep to the sounds and shadows of the television. There was still an oppressive heat in the air from a fight the two had had earlier in the day. He found out about some money she had given to her no-good brother. He wasn't working to support her goddamn family. The muthafucka better find a job. He didn't give a shit if he had been laid off. He had hit her and she must have tried to fight back because Eddie heard rumbling sounds. The floor was shaking. So he crawled under the cover on his bed – in the middle of the day. He had learned long ago that it was futile to try to stop the fights. The first one of them who could get his hands on you would knock you out of the way. Even she would, and she was always getting the worst of it. He knew that she was probably trying to make sure that he didn't get hurt, but he also saw her refusal to allow him to help her as evidence that she had feelings for his father that could not be easily explained – and somewhere beneath the confusion of it all was love. And when he was peeking over the wall to see what things looked like after the dust settled, he saw her pause while chopping the onions. She glanced into the living room at his father. She glanced back at the knife she was holding in her hand. Then she looked back at the figure who was there only in the corner of Eddie's eye. He couldn't stop looking at her. Her hand, in a tight-fisted trembling motion, raised the knife. Her whole body seemed to shake with hatred. She took a step toward the living room. Eddie watched, as if watching a movie that he was not a part of (he didn't know these people), paralyzed with fear and anticipation. Lord, he was thinking. This is what it has been leading to all along. There is no other way for it to end. (She took another step.) She must, she must. He could feel his heart tapping softly but quickly against the wall. She must, she must. Then – it was as if someone had pulled the plug – she stopped moving. Her shaking stopped and her body went limp. She collapsed to the floor. By the time he had pulled himself from the wall, waiting for it all to start again, to come back on, and made his way into the kitchen, his mother was already working her way back to her feet. He never let on that he had seen her; he said he had heard a noise. They both looked into the living room, but his father hadn't moved.

She loves him and she hates him, he feels, listening to the television, tying his shoelaces. It's just so fucked up. He doesn't want to be like them. He doesn't want to be anything like them. (He remembers how Marcus used to say how much he hated them when he was still at home. But Eddie doesn't hate them; he hates the way they are together, the *thing* they are together. He loves them – passionately. So does Marcus, he prefers to think.) But how is he to avoid becoming like them? Just tonight he told Betty he loved her. And what's more, he actually meant that shit. That's the scary part. That's probably the first step toward ending up like James and Dorothy in there. Betty already has him confused, too. Why does it have to be so complicated? He told her how much he really loved her and all she wanted to do was hug him. It doesn't make sense to him. Don't they know that sometimes you just have to have it? That if you get that close to them you just have to have it? Don't they know that sometimes your dick just gets hard and it won't go down until you have it? Nothing will bring it down but pussy. Pussy, pussy, pussy. Isn't that what it's all about anyway? Isn't that the way God planned it? He must have planned it that way, because that is exactly how it is. That's the way it is and there isn't a damn thing wrong with it.

So fuck Betty! (Please, Betty.) If she won't give it to him, he'll just get it somewhere else, he'll just find someone who will. (He can do that now; he knows how.) Fuck Betty. (Please, Betty.)

His fingers lock in the loops of the laces, and they pull in opposite directions to tighten the strings into a pretty bow.

There.

: 0 8

AND HE WAS 18 YEARS OLD...

HE IS on his mark, he is set... he is on his mark, he is set... he is on his mark, he is set. But what is taking so long? Why doesn't that fat sonofabitch shoot the gun, start this race! Everyone is waiting, waiting, waiting. The sun is kickin. It's already burning up, even this early in the track season. His body is covered with beads of sweat. He feels as though he has just emerged from a misty sauna. His muscles are still aching from the leg he ran on the 880-yard relay. And now here he is about to run this 100-yard dash. He doesn't mind, though. It's his favorite race. When he hears the gun, his muscles will automatically spring to action. He can almost feel the breeze that will flow smoothly over his face and arms and legs. His spikes will rhythmically splash cinder behind him and there will be cheering from the bleachers to his right.

This is his favorite meet of the entire year. The Jacob High School Relays. He likes it partly because it takes place at his school and he gets to show off in front of his friends. Everybody knows how good he is, how fast he can run, but they really believe it when they can see it with their own eyes. And he likes the meet because the competition is always tough. This year two teams from Beaumont and a couple more from Houston are here. These brothers can move too – and they know it. The one from Houston in lane two, the one who won the third qualifying heat with a record 9.8, is wearing a bad-ass pair of spikes. They're navy blue with a fluorescent orange swish on the sides. When Eddie told him how cool they were, he just sort of shrugged his shoulders and jogged on. A real snotty muthafucka. Still, Eddie promises himself to remember to ask Coach Tillis about getting him some new spikes before too much of the season passes. The competition is good, but it isn't frightening to Eddie. It only makes him run faster. When he ran in the first heat to qualify for this dash final, he finished in front of two runners who both had been timed before at under ten flat. Eddie ran a 10.1 to beat them, only two tenths of a second off his best time. He had clenched his fist high above his head as he crossed the finish line – partly for the crowd, but mostly for himself. He has to keep proving to himself over and over again how good he is at this one thing. No one can take this winning feeling away from him. Whenever he experiences it, he makes sure he relishes it. He can't tell when he'll stop winning. The winning could end today for all he knows – but not if he can help it.

He likes the sweaty smells mingling with all of the oils the runners use on their legs and the Icy Hot they rub themselves down with. He knows he'll never forget the smell of Icy Hot. Before basketball season is over and even before track practice begins, he can already smell it. It comes every year with the robins, like clockwork. His rubdown is starting to wear off now; he can tell that his muscles will be tense as soon as this race is over. He'll have to have another rubdown before he runs the mile relay, the race he hates. He has to run a quarter of a mile, and that just isn't his best distance. But since Coach really doesn't have anyone better to run the race, Eddie goes along with it. He usually runs the third leg of the relay. "Stick!" That's what you say while you are jogging around the track practicing handing off the baton in a team of four. "Stick!" you yell to the man in front of you. And he will reach his hand straight back toward you in a quick motion and you slap the baton firmly into his palm. During the race, he grabs it and he's off. There are teams on the infield going through these motions now. He's concentrating on the path in front of him and waiting for the sound of the gun, but he knows they are there. Some of them are in the periphery of his vision.

And there – well, what do you know (there he goes!) – also in the periphery of his vision, at the end of the field where the finish line is placed, is the high jumping pit. (From Eddie's perspective the pit is not far from the center of his vision, really.) He *sees* the action there, though it is his race that is commanding his attention. He sees it all. He sees Malcolm, back arched over the bar. It is a perfect pose, something to behold. Someone should take a picture. The bar must be set on at least six feet, eight inches. Malcolm is suspended high up in the air. When the man said "On your mark" just a moment ago, Malcolm was running toward the bar, making his approach. And when the man said "Set," he was planting his foot for takeoff. Now he is in this perfect pose. Not on his way up, not on his way down. Just hanging there gracefully. Malcolm, Malcolm, Malcolm, Eddie thinks. It's such a great act you have, the way you have all of these people convinced that you're just another high jumper. Boy, you're something else, hanging up there in that red tank top and those ballooning blue shorts. You really have them fooled. But not me. No, buddy. Not me. You see, I was there in the backyard with you sitting in the oak tree. I was there. I know all about your fantasies. I know all about your dreams. I'm on to you. You may have the rest of them fooled, but you can't fool me. Not me. Not your brother. You ain't just jumping. You think you can fly, muthafucka. You think you can fly. I know all about you and your flying Africans and how they could escape and be free. I know all about it. You told me, remember? I was the one you told in the oak tree. And I never told anybody else. It was our secret. I was scared they'd laugh at you. But look at them. Nobody's laughing at you now – and you're flaunting it right in front of their faces. And they're not laughing – they're cheering. I'm cheering too, Ace. You've got it now. Hold it. Just hold it right there. Don't come down yet. Hold it. We believe, we believe. I believe. Show me, Malcolm. Will you show me how to do it? I believe you. I want to come up there. Forget about this stupid race. I don't care about it. It's a bunch of bullshit, anyway. Like I really need another trophy or medal or whatever crap it is they're giving away this time. I want to come up *there*. Will you show me how? Please. I want to fly. I want to feel under my arms the force you talked about, the force that carried you in your dreams. I want the feeling that is like smelling freshly baked bread. I want to soar at night. I want to fly, Malcolm. What is the secret? Tell me. Show me. I am on my mark, I am set. Show me *now*. I want to fly. I want –

Pow!

The race begins, and Eddie sees (oh, no) Malcolm falling. Eddie runs.

AND HE WAS 34 YEARS OLD...

HE IS looking into Almeta's eyes. He was walking around the neighborhood in a drunken daze (what time is it?) and he saw a bright green scarf on the ground at her front gate. He knew she was there as he bent down to pick it up. He could feel her eyes. When he went for the scarf, he lost his balance and fell to his knees. The ground was wet. Maybe this was dew and it was morning. Or maybe the dampness was simply from a light rain. But his knees were cooler than the rest of his body. He thought he heard birds singing, but that could have been his ears ringing from the fall or from the impending hangover. He managed to grab the scarf with his right hand. And bringing himself up from his knees and into a partially crouching position (one knee was still touching the ground), he flicked his wrist and the scarf, quivering like a flag, caught his eyes. So he looked up to see it and to see at a distance resting atop the shaky line drawn by the waving scarf, staring deeply into his eyes, the eyes of Almeta. So he is squatting at her front gate looking into her eyes.

ALMETA: So at last we meet.

EDDIE: At last.

ALMETA: The day after the most painful day of your life.

EDDIE: The day before the most poignant day of yours.

ALMETA: And you are everything I knew you'd be.

EDDIE: And so are you.

ALMETA: I remember once you drove down the street past my house and you were afraid to turn and look at me.

EDDIE: I remember.

ALMETA: You and she had had a fight and you were trying to get away and be by yourself for a little while. And when you drove past in that old car you used to have, you refused to look at me.

EDDIE: I remember.

ALMETA: And then you turned onto Vincent Road.

EDDIE: I remember.

ALMETA: I knew you'd pass me by without looking up. I knew it.

EDDIE: I thought you knew everything then. All of my secrets. I thought you knew exactly who I was.

ALMETA: But, of course, I didn't know anything.

EDDIE: Yes. Now I know. I had no reason to fear you. Only now do you know everything. But I know everything, too. So I have no reason to fear you even now – and, really, I am not afraid.

ALMETA: Good. And I am not afraid either. We are equals here. Let us say what we have to say to each other.

EDDIE: I would like that very much.

ALMETA: Well, now I know what you might have shown to me

146

that day had you looked up. You could have let me see you running on a beach with your father and how you came to respect water as a force. This I see now. Just as I see you standing in the doorway on your way to the fence at the edge of your backyard on your way to feed Princess. I feel good watching you there. I could kiss you there. I am whispering into your ear; later, you make a toast to the world because you are happy to be alive. And there you are sitting in that restaurant with Betty, Pam, and Malcolm, wondering. And I see you flipping through the pages of a magazine. I see the subscription slip fall out and land in your lap. I see you crossing the street and popping your fingers and feeling like one of the Temptations. I see you at the starting line of the 100-yard dash waiting for the race to begin and watching Malcolm, feeling his life and then suddenly seeing him falling – when no one had seen him fall – to his death on the floor of the shop at the refinery. Yes, I see you with Coco. And I even see you on a park bench resting quietly with a mosquito on your cheek.

EDDIE: And I see you and your brother Gerald playing in a field of cotton. You are wearing a gray dress and there are pink ribbons in your hair.

ALMETA: Easter.

EDDIE: And you fall and cut your hip on a piece of iron. I see you picking cotton with your family and you, feeling like the dead grandmother you never met, hum a song you've never really heard. I see you hanging a white sheet in your backyard. You love the way the wind is blowing the sheet wildly. You pretend you have a boyfriend and that you are whispering into his ear. You blow a kiss to the sun because you are glad to be alive. I see you eating a piece of fried chicken at a table across from your two children, Paul and Sandra. And I see you hammering a nail into a wall in your bedroom because you found a framed print at K-Mart with a beau-

tiful little black girl in it who reminds you of your grand-
daughter, who lives in California with your daughter. I see
you reaching for your Bible because you want to be close to
it and look at the pages, though you cannot read them.
Looking into your eyes, I see yesterday.

ALMETA: And I see tomorrow.

EDDIE: And I see tomorrow.

ALMETA: And I see yesterday.

EDDIE: Looking into your eyes.

ALMETA: So at last we meet.

EDDIE: At last.

ALMETA: The day after the most painful day of your life.

EDDIE: The day before the most poignant day of yours.

ALMETA: Yes, I see her standing there in that living room and
you making your last plea.

EDDIE: And I see your brother Gerald knocking on your door.

ALMETA: I hear your voice: "Baby, I love you." That's all you
keep saying.

EDDIE: Gerald knocks three times, but there is no answer.

ALMETA: "Baby, I love you" is what you keep saying.

EDDIE: He knocks harder.

ALMETA: I see her motioning for the children to go out the door.

EDDIE: I see him looking around.

ALMETA: The children walk past you.

EDDIE: He reaches into the mailbox.

ALMETA: She turns away from you.

EDDIE: He removes a key.

ALMETA: She takes a step.

EDDIE: He puts the key into the door.

ALMETA: She stops.

EDDIE: He turns the key.

ALMETA: She turns.

EDDIE: He turns the knob.

ALMETA: She turns away again.

EDDIE: He pushes the door open.

ALMETA: She steps through the door.

EDDIE: He steps through the door.

ALMETA: You watch her.

EDDIE: He sees you.

ALMETA: She is gone.

EDDIE: You are dead.

ALMETA: Yesterday.

EDDIE: Tomorrow.

ALMETA: The beginning.

EDDIE: The end.

ALMETA: The end.

EDDIE: The beginning.

ALMETA: I keep seeing you.

EDDIE: I keep seeing you.

ALMETA: All of you.

EDDIE: All of you.

ALMETA: Over and over.

EDDIE: Over and over.

ALMETA: Over and

EDDIE: Over.

ALMETA: Over

EDDIE: And over.

ALMETA: I am here right now looking into your eyes.

EDDIE: And I am looking into yours.

ALMETA: And when the wind blows that scarf an inch higher, blocking out our line of vision, we will still be looking into each other's eyes and seeing everything.

EDDIE: Seeing everything through each other.

ALMETA: Through each other.

The scarf catches on the edge of a breeze and flies up. He sees only a green scarf.

AND HE WAS 35 YEARS OLD...

HE IS counting to himself, counting years and realizing how oddly familiar this whole scene is. The television is playing and there is a basketball game on. That's just the way it was then. The picture on the screen is blurred in his eyes because of the tears. Yes, he is crying just the way he must be. The way he was then. There is this mess to clean up – just as there was then. He doesn't know what came over him to make him do this. He hasn't done this since he was a teenager. He's never had any reason to – at least not until now. Now the house is too big. It is a big empty hole, and he is alone in it.

But he remembers how, for a few seconds, he pretended she was here, how he made himself believe he was not sitting in this house alone. He was watching the game, and she was in the back in the bedroom. And then Michael Jordan, 23, got a rebound and headed up the court on a fast break. And at the same time Betty came down the hall. She was walking slowly, but she somehow got into the living room in an instant. There she was between him and the television. Then there she was going down, down, no longer blocking the television, and there was the sudden flash of excitement. There it was. It was really there, but Betty wasn't. It was there from all the angles, but she wasn't.

When had he seen all of this before? Maybe when he was twenty-six, or maybe when he was seventeen. It is prophecy – his own. Yes, he is a prophet after all, it seems. Prophets cry, and at least one of the tears he is shedding now is for this revelation: *He is a prophet.* Maybe each of us is a prophet, and maybe each of us weeps only upon the fulfillment of his prophecy, face to face with the confirmation of his own great power and of the utter helplessness of the soul: inevitability.

So he is alone. This is the way it was then. This is the way it is now. And this is the way it will be one day when he falls asleep on a park bench with a smile on his face, unable to feel the mosquito that has landed on his cheek to draw some of his last blood. He is alone, he is crying, he is counting sadly – but with a finger-popping song in his heart and that smile on his face, forever and ever.

AND HE WAS 17 YEARS OLD...

HE IS slipping and sliding inside Coco, on the verge of the precious moment. She is his first. At last, after all of the lies, it will be true. He won't be a virgin. God, it feels so good. To be free of the lie. To be inside her. And he is not clumsy at all. It is exactly as he thought it would be. Slipping and sliding. All the practice with his hands was not wasted. But getting here was so difficult, it seems. Now he knows that he was just trying too hard. Somewhere down the road he got nervous about it, began to choke under the pressure, and thought he would never find the girl who would let him do it. He started to panic, to come on too strong. The girls must have thought he was a complete fool. But now he won't have that problem anymore. He has learned how to do it correctly, just this afternoon. Coco was the perfect teacher – willing. What had he said to her? Oh, yeah. He said: "What kind of a name is Coco?" That was all he said. And when he said it, something clicked. He suddenly knew it: This was how he must make his play. It was something in his voice – something hoarse, something simple and unmistakably manly. It was a voice that teased but that, at the same time, demanded to be taken seriously. With his words "What kind of a name is Coco" he felt his problems were solved. Just use the right tone, he told himself, and they will know what you want. *Say* things the right way, and they will give you some. *Relax*.

His brother. That is who his own voice reminded him of when he said that to Coco. His brother on the telephone talking to girls, stretched out on the twin bed across from his own. Eddie would listen while Marcus talked his stuff and rhythmically squeezed his crotch. "How do you *think* I got your phone number, girl," and "If you wanna be that way, thas okay, too." That was Marcus. And that is what Eddie has been imitating badly since he was twelve. But it has never worked. It has never clicked – until today.

When he knocked on the door, he expected Betty to answer. He had told her at school today that he would stop by after track practice because he had something special he wanted to ask her. But it was just like her not to be there. (Coco answered the door.) Probably just to upset him. She has a way of doing that. He thinks seeing him upset is something that pleases her, so he forces himself to hide any displeasure he feels when she has done something that aggravates him. Coco told him that Betty had gone over to Martha's house right after school. Eddie told her to tell Betty he had come by and to give him a call as soon as she got home. He turned to leave, but Coco, who was standing halfway behind the door, reached out and touched him on the shoulder, saying that he could wait for Betty if he wanted to. She said her mother wouldn't mind, even though she was still at work and wouldn't be home until much later. Betty might be back soon, but, then again, she might not. He could wait and take his chances – if he wanted to. If he wanted to? Eddie had to fight back his instinct to say something inappropriate to Coco, to tell her that he was reading her signals loud and clear – if he wanted to? – yes, he did want to. He had heard that Betty's little sister might be giving it up, but he had never really paid too much attention to her. Maybe there was something to the rumors. Maybe there was nothing he could say that would stop her from giving him some, but he wasn't taking any chances. He would hold off with all the shit that had never worked before. He would politely accept this invitation to wait inside. She didn't have to know that he knew.

When the door closed behind him, his heart almost stopped. He felt this was the closest he'd been since he was eight and he and Tanya from California had hidden during a game of hide-and-seek behind Hanchey's Drugstore and kissed. Almost instantly, he was hard.

Coco led him to the living room, and he sat on the sofa in front of the television. She plopped down into a chair off to the side and let her legs fall open slightly. Eddie's mind danced as he tried to stop his eyes from exploring the dark shaded openings that were between her short short pink shorts and the milky brown skin of her inner thighs. He tried to keep his eyes on the television, where the local news was playing, but they kept darting back to the thighs. He knew that she knew he was watching her, but there was nothing he could do. He would try not to say anything stupid, to let her make the first move. This was his plan. But he wasn't sure how long he would be able to hold to it. He was already starting to throb, as if he had a second heartbeat.

She offered him a Coke, but he said he wasn't thirsty. He just rubbed the palms of his hands on his knees, letting the rough rubbing sounds his hands on his jeans made soothe him somehow. The repetitive movements calmed him as well, the way rocking calms a baby. She said she had seen him run at the district track meet last week and he was really fast. Maybe he would win state.

He said he would have to make it there first. That would mean he'd have to get through the regional meet. He said he thought he could do it, but he wasn't sure; he was only a junior. He had another year left. She said she would tell him something if he would promise he wouldn't tell Betty she told him. He said he promised not to tell Betty. Well, when she and Betty were at the track meet, Betty told her how much she loved his pretty, fine black legs. That was just how she said it. She said, "Ooh, look, Coco. Look at him. I just love his pretty, fine black legs." She wasn't looking at the race like everybody else; she was just looking at him and how fine his legs were. But he couldn't tell Betty she had told him. Betty would kill her. And, Coco said—she hadn't said anything about this to Betty at the time, of course—she liked his legs, too.

That was too much. He could handle the sly invitation for him to come inside. And he was even managing to control himself despite her sexy pose. But here she was telling him that he was fine, someone to be desired. It was too much. He wasn't going to be able to control it. She'd be lucky if she didn't get attacked. No, he wouldn't hold it in any longer. He *couldn't* hold it in any longer. He would have to come out and tell her that, yes, he did want to do it and that at this point she would have to want to as well—otherwise he would probably make a very ugly scene. He had to say something: "Say, Coco—" But saying her name, simply saying her name, made all the difference. It stopped him from saying, "Why don't we, you know, just go screw?" The name tapped twice softly at the back of his throat and cleared open a passageway for a husky chuckle and for "Coco—What kind of a name is Coco?" And this was when he knew. He suddenly *knew*. He was home free. It would be smooth sailing from now on.

She didn't know what kind of a name it was. It was just what they called her. He said cocoa was something you drank in the morning in the winter to warm your insides. She said, well, maybe that was why they called her Coco, too. Because she could keep you warm, too. He said it was too bad it wasn't cold outside.

She looked around and then said she knew about some people who drank cocoa all the time, all year long. And then she actually got up from her chair and walked over to him. She stood there staring down at him with a look on her face that asked him what he was waiting for. He couldn't believe his luck. This was it. This was finally it. The thought that he and Coco were about to betray Betty never entered his mind. He had only two thoughts in connection with Betty. One: She'd better not come home before he and Coco were finished. And two: He could ask her to the prom anytime.

Coco took his hand and he followed her to the bedroom she shared with Betty. They entered the room and she closed the door behind them. They were both silent as they stood staring at the double bed. It was decorated with a sky blue cotton spread that had colorful flowers embroidered on it. A large white teddy bear was propped up against the headboard. Next to it, in the crease between the two big fluffed shapes of the pillows was a pink rabbit whose long ears hung loosely along the sides of its face. A smaller bear, this one brown, rested atop the other pillow and it seemed to have staring eyes. Coco went over to the window and drew the blinds and closed the curtains, making the room go hazy with soft blue light. Then she carefully gathered up the animals and gently placed them in a chair next to the closet door. Eddie wasn't sure but he thought he saw her pat the rabbit on its head and smooth down one of his ears. Then she started to walk toward him slowly, almost shyly, and he felt a rush go through him that momentarily blinded him. He swallowed intentionally, trying to bring himself down to a normal level of calmness. He knew his first priority was simply to do it and enjoy it, but he also knew that he had to remember it all, in all of its beautiful blue sensual detail, so that he could tell it. He might have to change her name – maybe not – but surely he would tell it. He'd have to tell it. By the time she had reached him he knew he was in full control, that he had managed to reach a level of equanimity that would allow him to remember it all; in fact, he had reached a state of such strong detachment that, indeed, he would never, even if he wanted to, be able to forget it.

She reached up and put her arms around his neck. Eddie let his head descend slowly under the weight of her pull until their lips met softly. Then he felt her tongue glide between his lips and begin to move around inside his mouth, as if in search of something sweet. After a few moments she pulled back and lowered a few inches in height; she must have been on her toes. She placed her hands at his waist, gathered in her fingers the T-shirt he was wearing, and pulled it out of his pants and up to his chest in one single fluid motion. He then let his arms go up into the air as she pushed and pulled the shirt over his head and away from his body, letting it fall to the floor. His nakedness briefly gave him a chill, but she gripped her arms around his back and pressed the soft flesh of her face firmly into his chest, chasing the chill away. She stood in that position so long that Eddie began to fear that this was all she really wanted to do, to stand here in the darkness hugging him with her face in his chest. So, gently, he loosened her arms and led her to the bed. Sitting beside her on the edge of the bed, he unbuttoned her blouse. She seemed as interested in taking it all in as he was, maybe even more so. The way she kept watching his fingers so closely, the intensity with which she stared into his eyes. He wanted to smile, but her seriousness was making that impossible. He avoided her eyes; she was taking all the fun out of it.

They kissed for a while with only their tops off; then they moved to opposite sides of the bed and, with their backs to each other, undressed completely. They met each other again in the middle of the bed beneath the flowers of the blue spread. The kisses and caresses were brief now; he was insistent. He placed himself above her, where he knew he belonged, and took a deep breath. She guided him into her slightly but stopped; there was pain. Then she let him in a little more. He knew where he was and wanted to move more quickly, but she was pushing up at his waist to slow him down. He tried to hurry her, but she gasped sharply, so he let her do it at her own pace for a little while. But soon he was inside all the way. And then, it wasn't long before she brought her hands up around his neck. He had no trouble with the motions his body needed to make. It was easy, natural. Slipping and sliding. Slipping and sliding. "I once kissed a girl from California. . . . "

Inside Coco now, slipping and sliding. These are the motions that are leading him to the point. The motions that are leading him to the moment. The motions that have led him to it – so quickly. And because he has practiced so often using only his hand and a picture in his mind of Betty, and because, really, what kind of a name *is* Coco, as the moment arrives he is panting three little words into her ear: "Betty, Betty, Betty."

: 10

AND HE WAS 26 YEARS OLD...

HE IS standing watching the two runners leading this 100-meter dash cross the finish line together. He is happy. He is sad. He feels a smile on his face. He thinks he feels a tear rolling down his cheek.

So maybe he has done something wrong or will do something wrong. But, he wonders, has he ever done anything that he could have avoided doing? At this moment he is sure that he has not. Watching this simple race has somehow convinced him that he has not. And when he loses this thing that is dear to him, he only hopes he can then make himself know that the wrong thing he has done to bring about his own loss is the only thing he was ever capable of doing. If he can travel deeply enough into himself to get this message through, he will have found something special, hope fulfilled: a kind of freedom he can call his own. Yes, he thinks. That is it. I am deep enough *right now*. Hadn't he once known that he would someday be able to go far enough into himself to find this truth, his innocence? Not long ago (or was it some time tomorrow, the near future?), thinking about lying in a woman's arms, hadn't he known there would come a moment when he would prove to himself that he is not guilty? And here is that moment, at a time when he desperately needs it. Here is his truth – he is not guilty, he never was, he never will be – pushing an apology to his lips. Here it is reminding him that he must buy donuts for his daughter. Yes, the moment is here as he knew it would be. His freedom is here now. Here, now. He can never be anyone else, and there is no need for him to try to be. *He is, he* does.

But mingled with his joy is a sense of impending doom, because even though he knows these things now, he also knows that this moment is almost over. And when it is gone, his tiny truth will be gone as well. When this moment is gone, he will be helpless, unable to speak his case, forever silent in his own mind, to his own mind.

So he is groping for a way to hold on to it, though his efforts seem futile. The moment is receding so quickly. The boys have run their race. They are crossing the finish line – together. But so closely together that there is no way to tell which of them is the winner. How will they know which one is the winner? How will he ever be able to hold on to his tiny truth?

And almost before he can tell himself what he is thinking, yes, just as the hope that springs from that thought has begun to surge, he finds himself smiling into the flash of a camera.

Louis Edwards was born in 1962 and grew up in Lake Charles, Louisiana. He attended Louisiana State University, spent his junior year at Hunter College, and received a B.A. degree in journalism. He has worked as a graduate assistant in English at LSU and the University of New Orleans. Since 1986 he has worked for the public relations offices of the New Orleans Jazz & Heritage Festival and the JVC JAZZ Festival – New York. He lives in New Orleans.